TH
UNSEEN
PATH

ANN FLANAGAN

WESTBOW
P R E S S®
A DIVISION OF THOMAS NELSON
& ZONDERVAN

WestBow Press books may be ordered through booksellers or by contacting:

WestBow Press
A Division of Thomas Nelson & Zondervan
1663 Liberty Drive
Bloomington, IN 47403
www.westbowpress.com
844-714-3454

ISBN: 978-1-6642-0847-6 (sc)
ISBN: 978-1-6642-0848-3 (hc)
ISBN: 978-1-6642-0846-9 (e)

Library of Congress Control Number: 2020920054

Print information available on the last page.

WestBow Press rev. date: 11/19/2020

Contents

Prologue

SARAH AND HER sister, Ava, were giggling in the back seat of their mom's new car as it rumbled over the gravel road kicking up a cloud of dust. Their mom, Eliza, and their Aunt Fan were chatting happily in the front seat of the convertible. With the top down, they had to raise their voices to be heard.

"Mr. Jerrol gave me a really good deal on this 1935 Ford," Eliza explained to Fan. "He took ninety dollars off." Eliza laughed and said, "That brought the price down to five hundred which cleaned out my savings account!"

Aunt Fan smiled as she turned toward her "adopted" nieces in the backseat. "I'm so happy for you, Eliza. You've worked really hard and now you have your very own car."

Eliza lowered her voice, "If only the girls' dad could see us now. It's taken a long time but I finally feel that we're on our feet financially. Of course, the stock market crash didn't help. But God always takes care of his children, doesn't He, Fan?"

"Yes, He does." Fan had come to Longview, Texas, to visit her cousin who was more like a sister to her and to see Sarah and Ava who had always called her Aunt Fan.

The Ford rolled on through the beautiful countryside with cows grazing in pastures and tall pine trees lining the road. The four of them had worn their hats that tied under their chins to keep their hair from blowing in every direction.

"Sarah, I wish you and Ava would sit down," Eliza said as she glanced in the rearview mirror. They were on their knees looking out the back. It was hard to sit still when something so momentous was happening!

"Mama, there's a car coming behind us," said Sarah. "It's coming really fast!"

"It's okay, honey, he'll probably pass us," Eliza assured her thirteen-year-old daughter.

Sarah and Ava looked at each other with big eyes as they turned to sit down. It seemed like the car was barreling down on them and would run them right over.

Fan turned around and saw the encroaching car and started to suggest that Eliza pull over and let him pass. But her words were never heard.

Everything happened so quickly and yet it all felt like slow motion. Sarah would always remember the feeling of having no control over her body, as though she were a rag doll that was being tossed into the air. She and Ava banged into each other and briefly saw their fear mirrored in the other's eyes. Then their bodies were airborne.

Chapter 1

The Hope Chest

SARAH SUYDAM LIKED to walk home for lunch this time of year. The flowering trees and bushes were at the height of their beauty in Alabama. Her new secretarial job at Fair Pointe High School gave her a degree of importance. The comment Millie Ledoux, her co-worker, had made that morning somewhat marred that feeling of importance. Millie's very words had been, "How can you be eighteen? You look like you're only fourteen." Sarah knew her wide-set blue eyes, pale blond hair and full lips with very little make-up didn't help her look any older.

Fan Ferguson, Sarah's aunt had graciously taken Sarah and her younger sister, Ava, home to live with her in Fair Pointe after their mother was killed in an auto accident five years earlier.

For years, Sarah had listened to adults talking about their financial woes and Fan had explained to them about the economic crash of 1929. But she and Ava had never gone without. Aunt Fan had always lived a very frugal lifestyle. Much of their food came straight out of her vegetable garden and off of her few fruit trees. Her apple pies were the best.

Sarah knew nothing of her father's whereabouts, only that he had left them when Sarah was three, soon after Ava was born. Sarah's mother, Eliza, had to get a job to support them and had become a very good secretary for the Land Bank until her untimely death when Sarah was thirteen. Aunt Fan took the girls in and had always made them feel loved and wanted.

As Sarah rounded the back of Aunt Fan's, there was a man sitting on the back steps. "Hello, Mr. Barlow," greeted Sarah. "Does my aunt know you are here yet?" she asked.

"Yes, she knows. May God bless her!"

Sarah entered the two-story white clapboard home through the back door into the kitchen. "Can I help you with Mr. Barlow's meal, Aunt Fan?"

"Oh, here's his plate, Sarah. Do you want to give it to him?" answered Fan. She lowered her voice, "He's one of the few hobos that still come around. Most of them are gainfully employed again, thankfully."

After Sarah handed Mr. Barlow the plate of food and came back inside, she noticed that Aunt Fan looked worried. Her aunt wasn't one to show her emotions. "Is anything wrong, Auntie?" asked Sarah.

"I don't like to burden you with my problems, Sarah. But I am worried about your sister. She's too young to be dating Howard. He's three years older than she is."

"Well, he is older, but he seems nice. Don't you like him, Aunt Fan?"

"I don't really know him. They never stay here very long before taking off in his car for who knows where." Fan paused as if she were making a decision before continuing. "Sarah, when it comes to dating, there are two kinds of men in the world. There are the kind that take advantage of women and the kind who don't.

"You and your sister are opposites. I never worry about you because you have a good head on your shoulders and seem wise beyond your years. Your sister, on the other hand, likes to leap before she looks. She's infatuated with Howard and sees him as the mysterious older man. She likes to charm him and I think she's succeeded. Well, I've said enough," Fan commented as she began putting their food on the brightly flowered tablecloth.

"We both know, Auntie, that Ava has been strong-willed all of her fifteen years and it hasn't been easy for you. It takes the two of us to get her out of bed some mornings. Then she doesn't seem to want to go to school. You're right. All she seems to care about is being with Howard."

"Well, let's just keep praying for her, Sarah. How was your morning?" asked Fan.

"I've learned so much and I'm getting pretty fast on the typewriter. My shorthand is speeding up, also," replied Sarah. "I work with a new girl who moved to town recently. Her name is Millie Ledoux. I like her a lot but this morning she told me that I look like I'm fourteen. I felt humiliated. She does tend to speak her mind."

Aunt Fan laughed and a smattering of wrinkles suddenly appeared. "Someday you will be ever so glad that you have a young-looking face, Sarah."

"I suppose I will," Sarah agreed. "I need to find my birth certificate so I can prove to Millie and anyone else who wants to know that I am eighteen!"

Sarah noticed that Aunt Fan's smile suddenly vanished. Sarah was about to ask her about it but Fan quickly said, "Let's eat, shall we?" There was a plate of small sandwiches and some fresh fruit for them on the flowered tablecloth. They bowed their heads and thanked God for the food. Sarah had to eat quickly and get back to the high school.

As Sarah walked the half-mile back to work, she thought about Aunt Fan's comments about men and wondered how she knew so much about them. Sarah didn't know of any romance in Fan's life. Then her thoughts turned back to finding her birth certificate. Her mother's chest was in Aunt Fan's attic. She had heard Fan say that Eliza's important papers were in it. Sarah decided to take a look that evening.

At 5:30 when Sarah arrived home, her sister Ava called out a greeting to her. Sarah sat down in the cozy living room where

Aunt Fan was arranging freshly cut flowers. She loved having a display of them in the house. The two girls talked while Aunt Fan put the finishing touches on the flower arrangement and returned to the kitchen to get dinner on the table.

"How was school, Ava? Did Howard carry your books for you today?" Sarah winced as she suddenly remembered what Auntie had told her earlier.

They could hear Aunt Fan give a little snort in the kitchen.

"Oh, of course he carried my books. All my friends keep telling me that Howard is smitten," was Ava's modest reply.

"Ok, girls, come on, let's eat. This bacon is a real treat and the neighbor's chickens have provided a generous supply of eggs. M-m these freshly sliced tomatoes are making my mouth water." Sarah and Ava had learned to enjoy the garden-fresh vegetables that Aunt Fan always had on the table.

The girls continued their chit-chatting while they washed and dried the dishes. Aunt Fan sat in the living room near the radio listening to one of her programs. The news reported that a new air record had been set in a flight from Los Angeles to New York in seven hours and twenty-eight minutes. Fan told Ava and Sarah about it and wondered at all the new inventions and how quickly their world kept changing.

As was her habit at day's end, she retired to her porch to listen to the crickets and the sounds of the neighborhood. The sunlight was fading toward the west and Fan could hear parents calling to their children to come in. They would have to end their games of kick the can and hide and seek until another day.

After convincing Ava to do her homework, Sarah climbed the steep stairs to the attic in search of her mom's hope chest. It didn't take long to spot the old chest near the window where the last rays of sun were glimmering. "A place for everything and everything in its place," was her aunt's motto.

Sarah had brought a flashlight in case the bulb didn't burn brightly enough. As Sarah put her hand on the chest's handle to open it, she suddenly felt goose bumps. Inside were memories of her mother, Eliza, which brought tears to her eyes. *If only our car hadn't been rammed from behind five years ago.*

Her mother had taken Aunt Fan, Sarah and Ava for a ride in the car she'd recently purchased. Suddenly a car came roaring up behind them. Sarah could still see it coming and remember the violent impact she felt when their car was hit and careened off the road. It turned on its side, dumping all of them onto the ground. Eliza was the only one who'd been seriously injured. She died three days later from bleeding in her brain. The hit-and-run driver had never been found.

Before the accident Sarah had sometimes heard her mama softly crying after they'd gone to bed. Did she cry because she missed Sarah's dad, or were there other things that had made her heart ache? Sarah didn't know because her mom never talked about her problems.

Sarah had often wondered why her dad left them and what he was doing. Did he ever think about them? Did he even know that Eliza had been killed?

Sarah picked up a folder that said Important Papers and began to look through them. Soon she had her birth certificate in her hand. It said that Sarah Grace Suydam had been born in Longview, Texas, on July 10, 1922. Finally! She would take it to work tomorrow to prove to Millie that she was indeed eighteen.

As Sarah got up, another document slid onto the floor. Sarah bent to retrieve it and saw that it was her parents' marriage license. How interesting, she'd never heard anything about when they'd gotten married. Floyd had never been around to celebrate an anniversary.

Sarah glanced down to find the date they were married and felt the goose bumps again. Floyd and Eliza had gotten married in late December of 1921. Thoughts raced through Sarah's mind. She'd been born in July of 1922. Sarah felt a sickening feeling in her stomach as she put two and two together. *That baby was me.* Her wonderful mother had married a man who would abandon them. Had Eliza only married him because she was carrying a baby that would need a father?

Chapter 2

Floyd

AVA LOOKED UP from her desk as Sarah came into their bedroom. "Where'd you go, Sis? You look as though you'd seen a ghost."

Sarah plopped down on her bed and wondered how much she should tell her sister of what she'd just discovered. "Well, looking into mother's hope chest and seeing her things might make you look like you'd seen a ghost, too."

"Oh," replied Ava, "Well, what were you looking for?"

"My birth certificate so I can prove to people that I'm eighteen," Sarah could hear Ava chuckling as she descended the stairs to find Aunt Fan.

She desperately needed to talk with Aunt Fan. But would Auntie tell her anything?

Sarah joined Aunt Fan in the living room. "Aunt Fan," began Sarah, "I need to tell you something."

"Of course, dear, but you're making this sound rather suspenseful. What is it?"

"Well, I decided to look in Mother's hope chest for my birth certificate and I found it. I also found Mom and Floyd's marriage license. I noticed the dates . . ."

"Oh Sarah, I wondered how long it would be before you would make that discovery. I'm very sorry it happened so unexpectedly.

I wanted to tell you about that but it seemed there never was a good time. I was afraid this would happen when you mentioned your birth certificate."

"Well, Aunt Fan, could you please fill in a few more details for me? How long had they known each other when Mother knew that, well, that . . ."

"Let me see," Aunt Fan had a thoughtful look on her face, "where to begin . . . well, your parents first got together at a high school dance. Floyd seemed older than his years. I believe your mother was just your age at the time. Floyd was a handsome man and the girls always noticed him." Sarah sat mesmerized as she pictured the scene of her parents meeting. She'd once seen a photo of Floyd and thought he looked like a movie star.

"Floyd lived with an older couple that had raised him from the time he was eleven. I don't think he ever felt they really cared about him. His dad had struck up an acquaintance with the couple after he and Floyd arrived in Longview. Jacob, your . . . grandfather, told this couple that he was down on his luck and could they please take care of Floyd while he traveled to California, got himself a job and settled in. Then he would send for Floyd to join him.

"The only problem was that no one ever heard from Floyd's dad again."

"What about his mom, didn't he have a mother somewhere?" asked Sarah.

"His mother had died from pneumonia when he was only seven. So, as you can see, he didn't get a very good start in life.

"I think he loved Eliza, but his restless heart couldn't settle down." Aunt Fan paused as if lost in another world.

"Aunt Fan?" Sarah's voice softly broke into that world.

"Oh, I'm sorry, let's see, where was I? I remember Eliza writing to me to let me know how she'd tried to explain to you why your daddy wasn't around anymore. How does one tell a three-year-old something like that? After Ava was born, Floyd seemed overwhelmed and distracted. Perhaps he had some kind of emotional breakdown. Anyhow, he walked out of your lives one day."

"Poor Mama," Sarah softly said, "I would hear her crying sometimes in the night."

"Yes dear, I know. But she would want you and Ava to know that she loved you both with all her heart. She got the job at the Land Bank in Longview and became their best secretary. In fact, the Bureau of Land Management wanted her to move to Nevada for the Hoover Dam project. But Eliza decided that wouldn't be right for you girls and decided to stay in Longview."

"Do you know if my father ever found out that Mother passed away?"

"I don't know, dear. Maybe someday we will find out." Aunt Fan walked over and sat next to Sarah and put her arms around her in a rare display of affection. "Please know, Sarah, that we can't always understand why things happen the way they do, but we know that God can work all things together for our good if we will only trust him."

"Yes, Aunt Fan, I want to believe that. And thank you for taking us in and making us feel wanted. We've been very happy living here with you."

"Well, now, I really don't know what I would do without you and Ava. Tomorrow, you and Ava both have plans with your friends, if I remember correctly?" Aunt Fan questioned.

"Oh, right," remembered Sarah. "Cary is coming by for me at 9 and we're picking up another couple. We plan to hike and have a picnic at the park on the bay. I'm not sure what Ava and Howard are planning."

"Oh – they're not going anywhere by themselves in that fancy car of Howard's, are they?" Aunt Fan sounded very worried. She could understand perfectly what Howard liked about Ava with her wavy brown hair, vivacious personality and other assets she'd been endowed with. She wasn't the perfect beauty like Sarah, but her more unusual features all combined to make a most bewitching countenance.

"Um, they have before, Aunt Fan. I don't know," answered Sarah.

"Oh, I don't know what to do about that girl. Well, not to burden you with it."

"Please try not to worry, Auntie. Good night."

"Good night, Sarah, sleep well."

Chapter 3

Boyfriends

SATURDAY MORNING SARAH and Ava awoke to the smell of buttermilk pancakes grilling in the kitchen. Sarah looked over at Ava, who barely opened one eye before pulling the covers over her head. "Okay, sleepy-head," Sarah teased, "I'll just tell Howard you slept in when he gets here in 45 minutes."

"What? Forty-five minutes!" cried Ava. "What time is it?"

Sarah had grabbed her clothes for the picnic and disappeared into the bathroom down the hall. She thought of Aunt Fan's abhorrence of make-up and just brushed a little face powder on and applied a light coat of mascara. Ava didn't need any color enhancement, but she liked to darken her mischievous eyes and wear lipstick when she could get away with it. Usually her lipstick came out of her purse as she headed down the walk toward the street.

The sun shone through the lace curtains in the breakfast nook. Aunt Fan took her apron off and the three of them sat down. "Sarah was telling me last night about the picnic and hiking they all plan to do by the Mobile Bay today. What are your plans, Ava?" Aunt Fan hated to sound like a worried mother hen, but she knew Ava wouldn't volunteer any information unless she asked. She regretted the mistakes she'd made in her youth. She had higher hopes for Ava and Sarah.

"I think we are going to walk around downtown Fair Pointe. Later we might run over to see Sarah and her friends, maybe play some croquet."

Aunt Fan had asked Ava many times to stay in a group when she went with Howard. She sighed and decided not to repeat the vain repetition again. "Lord," Aunt Fan silently prayed, "Ava is in your hands, please guide her away from trouble."

Just then, they all heard the squeal of Howard's car stopping abruptly out front. "Howard has arrived," stated Sarah sardonically.

"Ava! I don't want you out after dark," called Aunt Fan to Ava's back as she flew out the door.

Sarah and Aunt Fan looked at each other as if to say, "What's a person to do?"

Sarah turned to do the dishes while Fan retreated to the porch with the newspaper in hand. "I'll watch for Cary for you from the porch."

The news articles about Europe were grim. Aunt Fan could see that the madman, Hitler, was still on the move, this time invading Belgium and France. Nevil Chamberlain had resigned as prime minister of England. All of Great Britain would now look to Winston Churchill to save them.

"You look very somber, Auntie, what's happening in the world now?" queried Sarah as she gracefully slid into her favorite rocker on the porch.

"Every day there's more bad news about Hitler's invasions in Europe. Where will all the madness end?"

Sarah couldn't even conceive of such a maniac. She'd heard people at work discussing the war and debating about how long it would be before the United States came to the aid of the Allies. But most of the talk at work focused on the current events happening at Fair Pointe High School. She'd graduated there herself the previous spring and the principal was happy to hire one of their brightest students. Sarah had taken the business courses of shorthand and typing in school and was well-prepared for the position.

12

Just then Cary pulled to the curb in his Ford Coupe. He got out and came up the flower-lined walk to the porch. Sarah's heart sped up watching Cary. He'd been her best friend for years since her mother had died. But now, it was becoming more than a friendship. Sarah admired Cary's jet-black hair and his darker-than-night eyes. She liked the dimple in his chin. Most of all, she liked his personality. He always seemed a step or two ahead of those around him.

Of course, he had found his way into Aunt Fan's heart. She liked the way Cary had befriended Sarah after her mother's death. Sarah hadn't been any beauty at the time, just an awkward fourteen-year-old.

"It's a beautiful day to read the news on the porch, Miss Ferguson. That is, if there's any good news to read," commented Cary in his glib way.

"Yes, you're right about the day, Cary, but I haven't seen any good news yet. I guess I'll have to go to the sports section to see how well the Fair Pointe Panthers are doing in baseball. Hopefully they're doing as well as you and your teammates did last year."

Cary was ready to launch into a memory of that wonderful season when Sarah quickly interjected, "Cary, it's almost ten o'clock. We have to pick up Doris and Jimmy and get to the park."

Aunt Fan watched the couple get in the car and go on their merry way. They made a very attractive couple. "Hopefully, youth won't be wasted in their lives," she thought.

Sarah did have a lot of common sense. Aunt Fan chuckled as she recalled what had happened to Sarah out in Hollywood two summers ago. She had let her go to Hollywood with her girlfriend's family. Betty's older cousin, Herb, was awestruck by Sarah's beauty. He had a friend who worked for the MGM studio as a stunt man. When Herb's friend met Sarah, he told her he wanted to introduce her to Bing Crosby. Aunt Fan couldn't help smiling as she recalled how adamantly Sarah refused to be introduced to Bing. With her blond good looks, she may never have come back to little Fair Pointe.

At the Mobile Bay Park, Sarah and her former classmates were having a jolly time. They'd all gone through junior high and high school together. The day wasn't unbearably hot and the girls' cotton dresses were nice and cool. They were hiking through the woods when one of the girls suddenly screamed.

There in front of her was a big bull snake slithering into the underbrush. The guys teased Rachel the rest of the day. "Rachel, that was just a big bull snake, it didn't have a rattle. They're harmless!"

"That is until they have a disagreement with a rattler," lectured Jimmy.

"You guys just leave her alone," laughed Doris. "She only did what any of us girls would've done if we'd been the one to see it first."

The group finally came to the top of the hill and saw the old cemetery that their classmate, Kyle, had been telling them about. They walked around through the gravestones reading the inscriptions. "All these names are French," Kyle pointed out.

"This one reads, 'Claire Louise Sicker,'" said Betty, Kyle's girlfriend.

Rob came over and looked at the headstone. "That's not the right pronunciation. S I C H E R is pronounced Seashay. This land used to be owned by France," he explained. "Look! The dates go as far back as the 1700's."

"Well, I guess I'll just have to take some French classes," laughed Betty.

Jimmy added a little more history. "We've just been studying about France owning what we call The Louisiana Territory until we purchased it in 1803. Remember the history lesson Mr. Tuxbury gave us? Dauphin Island was the French capitol."

"Jimmy, when are you going to get your teaching degree?" teased Cary.

"Okay, okay, just because I'm more intellectual than the rest of you, rub it in, rub it in." They all laughed.

On the way back down the trail to the Bay, Sarah and Cary were out in front of their group. Sarah noticed a couple sitting on one of the benches under a huge live oak tree. Several benches encircled the majestic tree.

"Cary," said Sarah, "Do you see that couple over there? That looks like my sister and Howard. And he just kissed her!"

"Yes," replied Cary, "That's them all right and I believe he did steal a kiss from her."

"She's way too young for that kind of thing," spoke Sarah in a concerned voice. "I'm going over there right now."

"Okay, try not to embarrass them too much," was Cary's admonishment.

Ava and Howard had their backs to Sarah as she approached. They heard the sound of voices and laughter from the group coming their way and Ava turned around just in time to see her sister arrive.

"Oh! Sarah! I didn't expect to see you here," Ava spouted. She had a nice rosy blush on her cheeks. Howard looked quite uncomfortable himself as he stood and turned toward Sarah.

"Okay, you two, I'm not here to ruin your day. But Cary and I both saw you kissing. Howard, my sister is too young to be kissing boyfriends and you should know that." Howard looked down at his feet and didn't know what to say.

"Sarah, you have no right to barge in on us and tell us what to do," argued Ava.

"Ava, unless you want me to report this to Aunt Fan, you two better come with us right now," was Sarah's firm reply.

Ava knew her sister and knew that Sarah would do it. Aunt Fan would probably lay down the law and refuse to let Ava see Howard anymore. "Okay, okay, Sis. Come on, Howard, let's join them."

Cary had made sure Sarah, Ava and Howard didn't have an audience and had kept the group moving toward the bay. The three of them soon caught up.

The rest of the afternoon sped by with good food and a round of croquet in the park. The guys got up a game of baseball so they could show off their talents to the girls who never stopped talking while they cheered them on.

The sun was beginning to set as they all headed to their cars. Ava reluctantly got in with Cary and Sarah, having said goodbye to Howard. She knew there'd be more discussions with both her sister and Aunt Fan. *If only they would leave us alone.*

Chapter 4

Visit to Tallahassee

SARAH WAS SO excited – today she and Millie were driving to Tallahassee and staying two nights with a friend of Mrs. Ledoux's. Millie's mother had described Helen Lawrence's lovely two-story house just a few blocks from the capitol and the girls couldn't wait to see it. Sarah and Millie planned to ride the trolley to see the sites. Sarah decided to do some window shopping, knowing her pocketbook wouldn't really make it possible to buy very much.

"I plan to do more than just window shop," exclaimed Millie. "With the Florida State College for Women in the heart of our capitol, I've heard that the shops have the latest dress styles from Paris." She would splurge and worry about the consequences later.

"Helen is a very interesting person," explained Millie as they rode along the two-lane highway in Millie's car. "Her husband brought her over from France twenty years ago. They met and fell in love when he was working overseas for an auto manufacturing plant. Helen grew up in a very wealthy family. Her husband, Clyde, had a managerial position in the company and was able to offer Helen a life to meet her expectations.

"Mother told me they host events for young people to fill the void of not having their own children. Did you tell Cary about the young military men from Eglin Air Force Base and the young ladies that will be there from the college Saturday evening?"

"Yes," replied Sarah, "I told Cary about that and he teased me about meeting some handsome pilot who would sweep me off my feet. I'm glad he's not the jealous type like Margaret's boyfriend, Rob!"

"Oh right," answered Millie. "I heard him giving Mags the fifth degree at the picnic a few weeks ago. He didn't know I was in earshot, I guess. Having a guy like that around could be a real pain. Besides how does he know to be jealous unless he knows what he'd do himself if the tables were turned?"

"Wow Millie, you are sounding wise beyond our years," laughed Sarah. "But, you know, I think that's true which makes me doubly glad that Cary isn't like that."

"And that's one reason I plan to stick with John," confided Millie. "I think he plans to ask me to marry him soon. I hope he doesn't wait too long or we might not get to spend much time together."

Sarah knew the grim war being fought in Europe was on everyone's minds these days. She took a turn behind the wheel after the girls had stopped to enjoy the picnic Aunt Fan had packed for them. Sarah never tired of seeing the live oaks and long-leaf pines that lined either side of the highway. Driving through the "green avenue" as she liked to call it always gave her a thrill.

Finally, the buildings of Tallahassee came into view and Millie directed Sarah to Helen and Clyde's home. Sarah pulled through a fancy, wrought-iron gate and gazed up at the elegant home where they would be staying. "Wow," she said, "what a place."

"Yeah," replied Millie, "and mother said they lived in a mansion before the crash in '29."

"This looks like plenty of luxury for me, pal," responded Sarah.

A prim and proper maid opened the door to them and informed them that Mrs. Lawrence would be right with them.

Soon they heard the swish of Helen's taffeta skirt as she descended the stairs. Sarah was struck immediately by her regal beauty. Helen had white hair with shades of blond and a beautiful complexion that age hadn't seemed to touch. Her few wrinkles only seemed to add to her unusual beauty. She greeted the girls with open arms and instantly made them feel welcome.

"Ladies, I'm so very glad you could come," spoke Helen in her genteel voice. After the introductions were made and some pleasantries exchanged, Mrs. Lawrence beckoned them to follow her, "Come, let's get you settled and then I will show you around."

Sarah and Millie exchanged glances of wide-eyed excitement as they followed Mrs. Lawrence up the elegant stairway. "I thought you young ladies would prefer to share a room so you can visit to your hearts' content, so I've put you in the Magnolia room."

They entered a room with two canopied beds. French doors opened onto a balcony. Fancy iron ornamentation enclosed the balcony and left the view open to the garden below. The colors in the room were green and white and the furnishings were more beautiful than anything Sarah had ever seen. The Chantelle dresser was in pearl white. On one side of the room was a door that opened into their own private bathroom. Millie felt like she was dreaming. There was a spacious closet where they could hang their dresses.

The girls talked excitedly as they unpacked their bags. "Come on," said Millie, "I can't wait to see the rest of the house."

Millie and Sarah oohed and awed as Mrs. Lawrence showed them around her elegant home. In the back yard, Mr. Lawrence was speaking with the gardener. Helen introduced Millie and Sarah to her husband, Clyde. The gardener busily continued to plant flowers around the base of the oak tree in the center of the yard.

The yard had a path that meandered through colorful shrubs and flowers under a canopy of oak leaves. Sarah thought it was perfect, with just the right amount of tree foliage, not so thick as to hide the sunlight.

"Well, ladies, let's go inside and see what Molly has prepared for our dinner, shall we?" invited Mr. Lawrence.

After they were seated and Mr. Lawrence had asked the blessing over the food, he asked Millie about their plans for the next day. They had decided to do a city tour in one of the horse-drawn trolleys. Afterwards they could stroll around and go inside some shops and hear some of the jazz bands that played on the weekends.

"I think that's the perfect way to see the city on one's first visit," added Mrs. Lawrence.

Just then Sarah looked out the window and noticed the gardener looking in. His face was shadowed by his hat in the fading sunlight. But Sarah had the distinct impression that he was staring at her. She felt her skin go all prickly and then he turned and walked away.

The next day, Sarah and Millie had a glorious time exploring the capitol building, strolling through the city's lovely gardens and browsing through the shops. Before they knew it, the day of site seeing, shopping, eating and listening to the happy sounds of the jazz bands had come to an end. "We will have to do this again, Sarah," Millie said. "One day just isn't enough, is it?"

"You're so right, Millie." The girls had used their time together to inform one another of their hopes and dreams. Both the girls were expecting wedding proposals in their near future.

Sarah told Millie how she and Cary had been best friends for years. Cary had always teased her that she would be his wife someday. Sarah had always laughed and put him off. But that had all changed when Cary had to have an unexpected surgery that almost took his life. In those hours when Cary's life hung in the balance, Sarah knew how much she loved him.

The Lawrence's home was a flurry of activity when Sarah and Millie arrived. "Isn't it nice, Sarah, that we can just relax and enjoy the evening getting acquainted with people our age and not have to worry whether the men will find us attractive or not?" philosophized Millie.

"I totally agree, Millie. No pressure is what I like!"

Soon the grand old house and yard were filled with music and a myriad of voices, some laughing and others in more serious dialogue. Most of the young people had already met since they'd been coming to the Lawrence's for several months.

Everyone was very friendly during the delicious dinner. The ladies talked about their college activities and some, like Sarah and Millie, were employed. The servicemen shared some of their stories of life at Eglin. A young man in uniform told about one of their nights sleeping in the open air during boot camp. "In the middle of the night, one of the guys says to the drill instructor, 'Hey! Sir!!! There's a snake in my bag.' And the D.I. calls back, 'Permission granted to get out of your bag!'" It seemed the laughter would never stop.

After dinner, Sarah and Millie were sitting on the back patio waiting for the next game of croquet to begin when a young gentleman suddenly joined them. He introduced himself as Thomas and began to ask them all about themselves. His friendly, casual manner put them at ease and the three of them were soon deep in discussion. Eventually the talk of whether the U.S. would enter into the war came up.

"World War I was supposed to be the war to end all wars, ladies, but here the world is again with another large-scale war on its hands," declared Thomas.

"I notice you're not in uniform. Are you from Eglin Air Force Base also?" asked Sarah.

"I'm not at Eglin, ladies. My parents are friends of the Lawrences so that's why I'm here," explained Thomas. "I will be doing my part stateside. My father owns a trucking company that is already transporting metal to Gulf Shipbuilding in Mobile. They are one of the busiest shipbuilding ports in our country."

"I see," replied Sarah.

"Okay," announced a young man who was calling for the next group to play a game of croquet, "who wants to go this round?"

Thomas, Sarah and Millie were joined by a serviceman for the game. The four of them were immediately laughing their heads off at the missed shots. The yard was aglow with the long rays of sunlight coming through the great oak tree and the day could not have ended on a happier note.

Before everyone began to leave, Thomas pulled Sarah aside and asked if he could write to her and stop and see her when he drove a truck through Fair Pointe. "Oh Thomas, I'm sorry, I have a beau in Fair Pointe, and we've been seeing each other for a long time," Sarah explained.

"Aha," smiled Thomas, "I didn't think it was possible for such a beauty to be available. But, Sarah, I'll give you fair warning that if you ever are available, I will mysteriously appear to sweep you off your feet." And with that Thomas tipped his hat and was gone.

"Well, ladies," asked Mr. Lawrence at breakfast, "how did you like all your new friends last evening?"

"Oh, we loved the evening, and everyone was so nice," Millie replied, "and we can't thank you enough for inviting us."

"It was our pleasure," said Mrs. Lawrence.

As Sarah and Millie were about to leave the next morning, Mrs. Lawrence handed their picnic basket to them which was now filled with goodies from Molly's kitchen. Clyde and Helen told the girls to come back any time and waved goodbye from the porch as they drove away.

Sarah mused over the events and conversations of the past two days as they drove along. One memory didn't seem to fit with all the others. She recalled the way the gardener had looked in the window at her. *Maybe he was just admiring the gala, but it felt like he was watching me. How very strange.*

Chapter 5

Changes

THE NEXT WEEKEND, Aunt Fan and Sarah walked home from church together and tried to keep the conversation positive. Both of them were thinking about Ava and wondering what the climax of recent developments would be. When school started up Ava became more stubborn than ever about getting up on time. Sarah had never seen Aunt Fan so ready to lose her temper. Sarah had noticed that Ava didn't want to go to church with them either. Her excuse that morning had been a tummy ache.

Labor Day weekend had been another fun time for Sarah and Cary and their friends. They'd done a clam bake on the beach at Gulf Shores and roasted marshmellows around the fire pit. Cary and Rob had entertained them with spooky stories as they sat back to enjoy the crackling fire and watch the stars grow brighter in the evening sky.

"Aunt Fan, it's uncanny the way I stumble across Ava and Howard. Last weekend at Gulf Shores, when we all returned to our vehicles, I could hear a couple having a heated argument. I recognized Ava's voice and walked over to them. Before she saw me I heard her ask Howard, 'What are we going to do Howard?' Just then Howard looked up and saw me coming. He signaled Ava to be quiet."

"We better brace ourselves, Sarah. I've had a feeling that Ava's life is spinning out of control," confided Aunt Fan. *So much like Eliza and Floyd.*

They finished their walk through the neighborhood silently, without their usual commentary on people's well-groomed yards or the occasional hello of someone whom they knew.

When they entered the back door, Ava had an apron on and was fixing a noon meal for them. It had been a while since Ava had treated either of them in any way. They glanced at each other in surprise. "Well, don't look so surprised, why shouldn't I fix a meal sometimes?" asked Ava.

Sitting in the dining room together almost seemed like old times before Ava had started spending every spare minute with Howard. The three of them carefully avoided any subjects that would end the pleasant time. Eventually when there were no more chit-chatty things to say, Sarah decided to talk a little about Pastor Redding's message that morning.

"Pastor Redding spoke on how we can navigate through these turbulent times and about how we should prepare for the future by studying God's word and memorizing some verses about God's love and provision in times of difficulty. Our country could go to war and life as we know it would change drastically." Sarah could almost read her sister's thoughts and wondered why she'd wasted her breath.

"I'm so sick of hearing about that stupid war, I could scream," retorted Ava. "How will you and I feel, Sarah, if Cary and Howard suddenly go off to fight some war thousands of miles away?"

Aunt Fan wisely kept her thoughts to herself. *If Ava were spending time with girlfriends instead of Howard, she wouldn't have to be thinking about such things. She will be sixteen in a few weeks. Oh, if only there was a good reason for Howard to disappear out of her life, at least for a couple years.* Memories of her own youth and giving her heart away to a handsome young man flitted across Aunt Fan's mind.

"Since you are determined to discuss serious matters, Sarah, I have something to tell you and Auntie," Ava thought she could hear her own heart beating.

Sarah and Fan looked at Ava expectantly and yet their eyes held a look of dread as if they wished not to hear what she had to say.

"Well, I, um, there's just no good way to break this news. Howard and I plan to get married as soon as possible." Ava rushed on before Fan could protest. "I know I have to be sixteen, Auntie, unless you will give us your consent."

"Ava, do you really expect me to condone your marrying Howard when you are only a sophomore in high school?" demanded Aunt Fan.

"Well, Aunt Fan, what else would you have us to do? Because, you see, well, we found out a couple days ago from the doctor that I'm carrying Howard's child."

The bomb Aunt Fan and Sarah had been expecting had just been dropped. But instead of an explosion, there was a momentous quiet filling the room. No one knew what to say. Ava began to cry. The little girl inside her wasn't ready to grow up yet but grow up she must. It was being forced upon her. Her impish smile and bewitching ways couldn't rescue her from this predicament. She'd done it to herself.

Chapter 6

Other Disturbances

THE QUIET LASTED the rest of the afternoon. No one was very hungry when dinner time showed up on the clock. Aunt Fan desperately needed something to busy her hands and still her tumbling thoughts. She made a fruit salad that she served with crackers and cheese and persuaded the girls to join her on the porch for an evening snack.

Ava knew her aunt and sister's silence wasn't to make her feel worse than she already felt. Even in this time of great shock and disappointment, Ava knew her aunt and sister would always love her and want the best for her. Ava had to admit to herself the relief she was experiencing since she'd unloaded her burden.

The three ladies kept their voices down, knowing that occasionally a few words wafted across the distance between porches revealing snatches of conversations. "Have you and Howard discussed what you want to do?" queried Aunt Fan. "You mentioned getting married, but have you considered any other options? You know, Ava, there are homes for unwed mothers. Once the baby is born, you could come back here and I will help you to care for the little one for as long as I possibly can."

"Auntie, I know you would do just that, but you see Howard and I are crazy about each other and we truly do want to be married," Ava had the dreamy look of young love written across her features as she spoke.

Sarah jumped into the fray, "Ava, how does Howard plan to support you?" Should I tell her now, she wondered, about mother and Floyd having to get married? Floyd apparently had felt plenty of frustration during those first few years of fatherhood. No, she decided, we already have enough issues on our plate right now.

"Howard works for his dad, Sarah. Of course, he'll continue to work on the dairy farm. Howard thinks we can build a small house in one corner of his parents' property," Ava explained.

"You and Howard seem to have things worked out, Ava," Aunt Fan interjected. "So, I'm guessing you two have already decided when to be married?"

"Yes, Aunt Fan. We had our first date almost a year ago, one day after my birthday. We'd like to be married at the courthouse on October 10. There's a little house not far from the Hamlin's farm that we can rent until some of the men get our home built."

"I don't mean to be crass," Sarah stated, "but your little one might really appreciate it if you were married as soon as possible. After all, he or she will one day see a birth certificate and figure it out."

"Now that sounds just like my wise older sister talking," quipped Ava. "And you know, I think you're right. I will talk to Howard."

Aunt Fan and Sarah exchanged looks and Sarah realized Auntie understood exactly why Sarah had thought of it.

Chapter 7

The Wedding

WORD GOT AROUND quickly that Howard Hamlin and Ava Suydam were to be wed on September 17. People could think whatever they pleased but the three ladies that abode together at 302 Washington Street weren't telling any secrets.

The ladies at their church decided they could quickly throw together a lovely wedding venue if they all worked together. Aunt Fan and Sarah had persuaded Ava and Howard to have the ceremony in the church. Pastor Redding had met with the couple and was satisfied they both were on the same page spiritually and there was no reason not to join them together as husband and wife. He knew there would be a lot of bumps along the way having gotten such a rocky start. But he would help them all he could.

Aunt Fan told Ava about her mom's wedding gown that had been hand sewn by Fan's grandmother. Ava liked the idea of wearing the gown that Fan would have worn if she'd ever gotten married. When Ava tried it on the beautiful gown fit perfectly. Ava was surprised that not even the waist band would have to be let out.

Howard's parents and Aunt Fan were getting better acquainted every day as they quickly readied everything for the wedding. Before they knew it, a little one would be calling all three of them Grandpa, Grandma and Auntie. It's not the way they would have chosen for their young ones, but they wanted them to get the best start possible.

The weather was beautiful the morning of September 17. It could be very hot that time of year in Alabama or it could be a rainstorm. But the day turned out to be a perfect 79 degrees in the shade. Ava had no one to give her away so Howard's Uncle James escorted her down the aisle.

The ladies had filled the church with flowers from their yards. Sarah and Cary thought Howard looked quite dashing in his black suit. He had the physique of a young athlete. His wavy, sandy-colored hair was combed back, and his blue eyes shone with expectation. Sarah thought he looked like a man completely smitten. He'd been around Ava long enough to know that she could be petulant if she didn't get her way. Perhaps his seniority over Ava would give them the advantage they would need in the days ahead.

Sarah thought about her own parents' wedding day and wondered if it had been anything like this. It amazed Sarah that such a beautiful wedding could almost magically appear in two weeks' time.

People milled about the Hamlins' large yard for the reception afterwards. Cary and Sarah wandered about visiting with their neighbors and school acquaintances. "Hey, you two," called Rob, "looks like you'll be next, am I right?" Cary and Sarah looked at each other and back at Rob and just smiled.

"Well, Sarah Suydam, I can't believe my good fortune," Sarah heard a male voice ringing in her ear. She turned and saw a familiar face and soon recalled meeting Thomas several months ago in Tallahassee. His blond good looks hadn't changed.

"Thomas, what are you doing here? I mean, I didn't know you knew Howard or Ava, my sister," Sarah replied. She wondered why she felt a warm blush come over her cheeks.

"Cary, this is Thomas. Millie and I met him at the Lawrence's in Tallahassee. Remember when Millie and I went there a few months ago?"

Cary had laughter in his eyes as he turned to Thomas and warmly shook his hand. "Nice to make your acquaintance," he said. "Any friend of Sarah's is a friend of mine."

As the two men struck up a conversation, Sarah couldn't help noticing how handsome they both were, yet in opposite ways. Cary was the dark, enigmatic type with a very noticeable dimple in his chin. Thomas was blond with strong Scandinavian bone structure. Both of them had an abundance of confidence and both enjoyed a good challenge. Once again, Sarah was so thankful that Cary wasn't the jealous type.

The three of them visited until it was time to see the bride and groom off in the Hamlins' shiny Buick. Howard's friends had tied cans to the back of the car and painted Just Married on the back window. Before Ava got in she stood up on the running board to toss her bouquet toward the crowd of young ladies. Ava smiled her impish smile and laughed as she turned around and threw the bouquet backwards over her head.

Sarah could see it flying her way and needed only to raise her hands and grab the bouquet. She laughed and felt herself blushing again as everyone cheered and clapped. Cary and Thomas stood on either side of her and she dared not look at either of them.

She heard someone shout, "Cary, old man, what're you going to do about that?" and everyone laughed. That is, everyone but Thomas. He was watching Sarah. His scrutiny made her uncomfortable.

Thomas turned to Cary with a challenge in his voice, "If you wait too long, old man, maybe someone else will turn her head." He took Sarah's hand and kissed it and doffed his hat toward Cary before strolling toward his sports car.

Cary gave his little laugh that always made Sarah want to ask him, "What are you thinking right now?" But he never would tell her.

The celebration was over. Sarah, Cary and Fan stayed and helped the Hamlins clear the yard and get things restored to order. Finally, the goodbyes were said and Cary drove the ladies home.

"My sister looked very happy, didn't she?" Sarah asked Cary in the front seat.

"Yes, they both looked very happy," replied Cary as he smiled into her eyes.

Aunt Fan hoped that this rite of passage would help Ava settle down and take life more seriously.

Chapter 8

An Unexpected Discovery

AUNT FAN WATCHED Sarah walk in the direction of downtown Fair Pointe and thought how much had changed in their lives just in the last few weeks. She hadn't allowed herself to analyze the tremendous relief she felt that Ava was no longer her responsibility. She had felt completely unsuccessful trying to direct Ava's life for the past five years since Eliza had been killed. But now that challenge was over, and she hoped that Ava would be happy as a wife and young mother. *Sarah will be gone, too, before I know it.* "Enough of all this introspection," she told herself and got up to do the breakfast dishes.

Sarah was doing some analyzing herself as she walked toward the high school to begin her workday. She realized that Thomas had never told her how he'd come to be at Ava's wedding. *Why am I meeting another young man that I am attracted to when I already know I want to be Cary's wife?*

How did my mama feel when she was deciding what to do after finding out she was carrying a child? Life can be so puzzling. Once again, her thoughts turned to the illusive memories of her father. Sarah tried to bring into focus the blurry image of a handsome, laughing man who had played with her and lifted her high up in his arms.

Sarah remembered a picture of Floyd that she had seen on Eliza's dresser. *It must be in the hope chest.* Once again she would open it and hunt for more of her past.

Sarah entered the front doors of the two-story brick school building and bumped into some classmates of Ava's. "Oh, hi, Sarah," they said as they quickly continued down the hall. A couple of them giggled and turned to look at Sarah as she watched them go. It made her sad to think that Ava's education was over. Young ladies who became pregnant did not continue attending school. It would cause too much discomfort for all parties involved. But Ava had made her choices and now she would live with their consequences.

Millie's welcoming smile was just the tonic that Sarah needed. "Hi there," said Millie. "John and I sure enjoyed Howard and Ava's wedding. Wasn't it amazing how it all turned out so beautifully?"

"Yeah, it really was," agreed Sarah. "Just shows what people can do when they all come together for a common purpose."

"It gave me some ideas of what I want in our wedding," admitted Millie.

"Why don't you come for dinner tonight and you can tell me all about it," replied Sarah. "Auntie and I aren't used to it being just the two of us yet."

"Good morning, ladies," the principal said as he came into the secretaries' domain from his office. "You will need to type these letters for the parents of the freshman students," and he handed a copy to each of them. "That's a lot of typing so have fun! There are brand new sheets of carbon paper if you need a new one." He smiled over his shoulder as he headed to the gym for the morning assembly.

Sarah gave Aunt Fan a call at noon to let her know Millie would be joining them for dinner. When five o'clock rolled around the two friends grabbed their hats and exited onto the tree-lined avenue. "I love this walk," said Sarah. "It gives me time to think and relax after a noisy day of clicking typewriters."

"I know," replied Millie, "and these yards are so beautiful. I wish my parents took more interest in making our yard beautiful with flowers and shrubs."

"Aunt Fan loves to do her yard work. And I'm sure you'll get a taste of her home-grown vegetables tonight."

For the rest of the walk Millie filled Sarah in on the things she wanted incorporated into hers and John's wedding. "John told me the other day that he really thinks we will go to war soon and he wants to wait for us to get married. He is so practical. I wish he were a little more of the romantic type," laughed Millie.

"I for one will be glad if Cary doesn't propose to me right now because frankly with all the upheaval of Ava suddenly being married and meeting mysterious Thomas has me befuddled," Sarah honestly admitted.

"Oh, Sarah, how can you doubt your love for Cary?" Millie was shocked. "He's always had eyes only for you and he's got everything going for him. Not only is he tall, dark and handsome but he has the personality to go with it!"

"I know, Millie, and I do care deeply for Cary. There's just too much to think about lately."

"You are an unusual young lady, Sarah. Most girls would snatch Cary up so quickly it would make his head spin," laughed Millie. "Maybe that's why he keeps coming after you because of the allure of the unobtainable."

Sarah laughed hilariously at Millie's psychology. "Oh Millie, you are so wise at times, but the way you put things does make me laugh."

Aunt Fan was scurrying around in her bright orange and red apron when the girls entered the back door. "Auntie, is that delicious smell what I think it is?" asked Sarah.

"Yes, it's your favorite - shepherd's pie. And I made a chocolate cake for our dessert since we have the honor of your presence,

Millie." Sarah loved Aunt Fan's natural gift of hospitality that always made people feel welcome.

After dinner Sarah and Millie did the dishes for Aunt Fan. Sarah told Millie that she wanted to find a picture of her dad. "Let's go up in the attic and look for the picture," Sarah suggested. The girls climbed the steep stairs that lead from the second floor into the attic.

"Oh, your aunt's attic is the cleanest one I've ever seen," noted Millie.

"Here's my mother's hope chest." The girls knelt on the braided rug in front of the chest. Millie's big, brown eyes looked as excited as Sarah felt.

"Sarah, I feel like we're looking for hidden treasure," Millie breathed.

Sarah opened the lid and began to carefully move her mother's things around. In the back corner of the chest she lifted a baby quilt. Underneath the quilt lay a small photo album. The girls turned around and sat with their backs against the chest. Fading sunlight came through the window.

"The relatives have always told me I look like my mom," explained Sarah.

Sarah passed the photos to Millie. "The resemblance is amazing, Sarah!" Millie could see it was certainly the case as she gazed at the few photos of Eliza.

"Another mystery, why did my mother have to die so young"? Sarah wondered aloud.

"I'm so sor-," Millie began to say when Sarah's voice suddenly cut in.

"Here it is, Millie!!!" She held the picture for Millie to see.

Millie's jaw dropped open. "What is it, Millie?" cried Sarah. You look like you've seen a ghost."

"Sarah, remember when we were driving home from Tallahassee and you told me how the gardener was staring at you from the porch? Well, this is the same man."

Sarah was dumbfounded. "Millie, what are you saying? How could you even know that? The sun was setting and his face was in the shadows."

"Yes, but you see, I saw him earlier. I was waiting for you to come back outside the first evening we were there. The gardener walked past me and tipped his hat. I saw him plainly. I know it's him, Sarah, unless he has a twin."

"But this was at least fifteen years ago," said Sarah. "How could you recognize him when he's that much older?"

"I don't know," pondered Millie, "maybe he has good genes."

Sarah didn't even laugh at Millie's funny explanation. They both were awestruck over their discovery.

Chapter 9

Deliberations

THE GIRLS SPENT the rest of the evening in Sarah's bedroom discussing the possibilities that this new information presented them.

"What should I do, Millie? What would you do if you were in my shoes?" asked Sarah. "I've always secretly clung to the hope that someday I would meet my dad and that he would put his arms around me and tell me how very sorry he is for abandoning us."

"Yes, but what if he isn't sorry?" Millie wisely cautioned. Millie didn't want to state the obvious to her friend – that her dad had seen her and skipped the opportunity to talk with her.

"And that would be more crushing than not meeting him, wouldn't it?" questioned Sarah. "But it must have happened for a reason, Millie. Maybe he wasn't sure who I was when he saw me," Sarah argued more with herself than with Millie.

Millie's big brown eyes had never looked so serious. She wished she knew what to say to Sarah. "If you want to pursue contacting your father, I will talk to my mom and ask her if she would call Helen, I mean Mrs. Lawrence, and ask her about their gardener. I think she and my mom were good enough friends that Mom could explain some of it and Helen would keep it between them."

"Yes, good idea and I will talk with Aunt Fan. I've never kept secrets from her, and I know she will help me know what to do."

Sarah hardly slept that night. Thoughts tumbled through her mind. She relived the scene in Tallahassee over and over. She imagined what Floyd's thoughts must have been when he first saw her that evening. *Did he somehow know for sure I am his daughter? Did he see mama the way she looked when he'd first met her? What if he thought she was still alive?* And on and on it went until the wee hours of the morning when Sarah finally dropped off to sleep.

She would have to wait until after work to talk with Aunt Fan. The hours dragged by as Sarah typed and ran errands and filed papers. Millie knew why Sarah looked so tired and the two exchanged many glances throughout the day that said volumes.

When the workday finally ended Millie and Sarah walked together as far as Millie's house. As they parted Millie said she couldn't wait to talk with her mom that evening. They agreed to pray that God's will would be done.

Sarah could hardly keep from running the rest of the way home. At five foot six inches tall she didn't wear high heels like so many of the young ladies. But Sarah knew every neighbor that saw her would wonder what in the world had happened that made her sprint through the neighborhood.

"Aunt Fan," Sarah cried as she came up the steps of the porch, "I have to tell you something. I've been waiting all night and all day to talk with you."

"Well I hope it's something good," quipped Aunt Fan. "I'm ready to return to normalcy for a little while anyhow."

Sarah knew Aunt Fan was as solid as a rock when it came to the ups and downs of life so she plunged in and told her about Floyd's picture and the gardener at the Lawrence's.

From the look on Aunt Fan's face, Sarah wasn't too sure she had done the right thing. "Oh, Aunt Fan, I know what Floyd did to my mom was very hard on all of us and I'm sorry to bring his name up. But I must try to get in contact with him."

Aunt Fan was quiet for a while. Sarah knew she had to wait for Fan to speak. Sarah could see the wheels turning as her aunt processed the information. Suddenly a resigned look swept across Fan's face. "Sarah, he's your father. If you want to try to contact him, you go ahead. But I want to warn you that he may let you down in a very big way. You are a grown woman now and I won't stand in your way."

Sarah ran up to her room and returned with Floyd's picture. "Here's his picture Auntie. Would you like to see it?" Sarah noticed Fan's hand tremble as she reached for the photo. But Sarah wasn't prepared for the look of pain that crossed Fan's countenance. It seemed that a myriad of emotions trembled on her aunt's face, and then the strong woman that Sarah had come to know and love was back in command of herself. She calmly handed Floyd's photo back to Sarah.

Up in her room, Sarah studied Floyd's picture for hints of who he really was. His eyes were unusual. They weren't big but they had a unique slant that reminded Sarah of someone. His features weren't the usual ones that people considered handsome, but he was indeed handsome. "Oh! Just like Ava," Sarah could see that it was the same kind of attractiveness that her sister possessed. His smile seemed almost like a little smirk.

Now she must wait to hear what Mrs. Ledoux would relate to her daughter, Millie.

Chapter 10

Millie's News

MRS. LEDOUX HAD assured her daughter several times that she did indeed try to call her friend, Helen, and had been informed of the Lawrences' business trip to Ypsilanti, Michigan. Mrs. Ledoux had requested that Helen call her when she returned. The house manager promised that Mrs. Lawrence would be given the message as soon as she returned. Millie and Sarah decided to put the hunt for Floyd out of their minds while they waited. At least, they would try.

The next morning Sarah drove to Ava's to get her mind off of things. "Oh, Sarah, I'm so glad to see you," exclaimed Ava.

"Well, are you going to ask me in, Sis?" The girls laughed as though they were playing house as they'd so often done as children. Ava and Howard had fixed the small rental house up very nicely.

Ava showed Sarah around the one-bedroom bungalow. "It's very cozy and clean, Ava," smiled Sarah.

"Well, I have plenty of time to keep it clean," admitted Ava. "In fact, by early afternoon I don't really know what to do with myself. I wish my girlfriends felt more comfortable when I see them. We don't seem to have anything in common anymore."

Sarah could readily understand Ava's predicament and felt a little sorry for her sister. "Well, when the little one is born, you will find yourself extremely busy," she said.

Sarah had intended not to mention the drama about their dad, but she soon realized that it wasn't a secret she could keep from her sister.

After she explained all the happenings to Ava and how Millie had recognized Floyd's picture as the same man they'd seen in Tallahassee, Sarah expected Ava to be excited. Instead Ava merely said, "Oh, Sarah, I have no memory whatsoever of that man and in a way, I don't ever want to meet him. After all he left us and didn't want us."

"But Ava, it's so strange that I just happened to encounter him. Don't you think that God might want us to meet our father?" Sarah asked.

"I don't know," was Ava's noncommittal reply. "Of course, I suppose little Harold or Julia might want to know both of his (or her) granddads."

Sarah decided to drop the subject. "Tell me about the cabin you rented for your honeymoon."

"Oh, it was so wonderful to stay at Gulf Shores. We liked the cabin and the weather was great for beach time every day. I wish we could have stayed longer but three days was all Howard could take off."

Ava suddenly looked like a frightened little girl. "Sarah, has Cary registered with the draft board yet? That's the first thing Howard did when we returned to Fair Pointe."

"Yes, he did last week. I think all the young men we know have registered."

"I just don't know what I'll do if Howard leaves me," bemoaned Ava.

"You like Mrs. Hamlin, don't you, Ava? And you know you can always come over to Aunt Fan's."

"Yes, I really do like Mom Hamlin. She's been very kind. She's going to teach me how to can the garden vegetables. Howard's sister, Nora, lives in Georgia. I think Virginia, Mrs. Hamlin, really misses her so maybe I can help fill that void."

Sarah was surprised to hear Ava express real concern for someone and thought that married life might be very good for her sister.

"Millie wants you to call her," Aunt Fan told Sarah when she returned home.

"Oh, maybe she has news about Floyd." Sarah quickly threw her purse and sweater down and went to the phone.

Aunt Fan waited on the porch. Finally, Sarah came out and joined her. Aunt Fan could see right away that Sarah was disappointed.

"Millie said that when the Lawrences returned from Ypsilanti, Floyd was no longer in their employ. The manager had hired someone to replace him. The only reason Floyd gave for leaving was that he had to travel to another state and didn't know when he could come back."

"I'm sorry you are disappointed so soon, Sarah, but maybe it's for the best. This is exactly what I would expect. Floyd saw you and probably was plagued with guilt. His only remedy for facing life's problems is to run."

"Well, Aunt Fan, you were right to warn me. Now I must once again try to forget my father."

"Come on," said Aunt Fan, "let's go listen to the radio for a while. That will get our minds off of our own troubles."

Chapter 11

War

THE MONTHS HAD flown by and John had asked Millie to marry him. On this cool December morning, they had announced their engagement in church. Fan and Sarah invited them to come over for Sunday dinner. Cary pulled up to Aunt Fan's house and hopped out to open the doors for Sarah and Fan.

Fan had roast beef in the oven, mashed potatoes keeping warm on top, freshly sliced tomatoes from her garden and only needed to boil the corn on the cob. The warm biscuits were ready to melt in their mouths. It was a festive occasion as they all sat in the dining room together. Even though war was looming in all their minds, no one cared to mention it. They discussed John and Millie's plans once they were married.

"Oh, Miss Ferguson," moaned Cary, "my stomach doth protest. It thinks this must be Thanksgiving all over again. Your cooking is delicious as always!"

Aunt Fan smiled and thanked him while the others were agreeing. "How about we retire to the porch to let our food settle," she suggested, "and we can have the strawberry rhubarb pie later."

"That sounds like a good plan, Aunt Fan," offered Sarah. Everyone helped carry the dishes to the kitchen. "Let's just leave these dishes to soak for now. I'll do them later."

"Sarah, your aunt has the loveliest porch around. She really has the green thumb to make all these flowers continue blooming this long," commented John.

"Hard to believe this is December," added Cary. "I've never missed the cold, snowy winters up north. I'm so glad Dad decided to take over Uncle James' pecan orchard ten years ago. And you all know the most important reason I'm glad," Cary took Sarah's hand as he spoke.

Just then, Aunt Fan came out looking breathless. "That was Marge on the phone, one of our neighbors. She said to turn the radio on. We are at war!"

Inside, Aunt Fan quickly crossed the living room and turned on the radio. They all gathered around and heard John Daly's voice, "The Japanese have attacked Pearl Harbor, Hawaii, by air, President Roosevelt has just announced. The attack also was made on all military and naval activities on the principle island of Oahu." They listened with somber faces to Daly's report. John Daly went on to say, "The details are not available."

When the broadcast returned to the regular scheduled program, Cary turned the volume down and quietly said, "Let's leave it on and listen – there'll be more news."

John and Cary looked at each other and their expressions said it all. Millie and Sarah looked at the men they'd come to know and love and knew what they were seeing. Everyone in the room realized that life had suddenly changed in a permanent, irreversible way and the courses of their lives would change as well.

Cary turned to John and said, "I wonder how long we have before we'll be called to active duty?" Sarah and Millie looked at each other trying to gain strength from the other. They knew in that moment they had to be strong and help their men as much as possible. They wouldn't give way to hysteria. Everything seemed to move in slow motion to Sarah.

Aunt Fan watched the four young people before her. Would the five of them ever stand in this room together again? She had been a teenager during WWI. Many of the young men she had grown up with left to fight and she never saw them again.

The following day, Congress declared war on the Empire of Japan. Work was suspended for Sarah and Millie. They wanted to spend every spare minute with Cary and John. The four of them drove together to get the things the men would need.

Everything happened quickly as time ran out like the sand in an hourglass. Cary and John, along with Howard, were scheduled to take the bus to Camp Blanding the next day, December 10.

Ava and Howard came by in the evening so Howard could say goodbye to Aunt Fan and Sarah. Cary and Sarah were sitting on the sofa holding hands. Sarah hoped Ava would be able to hold up. She didn't seem to fully understand the ramifications of Howard's going. Perhaps she wasn't ready to face the awful truth that he would be gone for who knew how long.

Aunt Fan remained quiet and supportive and assured the two men that she and the others would hold them in their prayers every single day. After Ava and Howard had gone, Aunt Fan took herself to bed leaving Sarah and Cary alone on the porch.

"Well," quipped Cary, "I guess I should have popped the question a few months ago!" He wanted their last moments together to be happy and as free from care as possible.

"Oh, Cary, my life will seem empty without you," Sarah softly said as she lay her head against his chest. She remembered what she'd recently told Millie about feeling confused. Now war had come and claimed her man. She suddenly knew she wanted to spend her life with no one else.

She could hear his heart beating and lifted up a silent prayer to God to keep that heart beating. "Bring him back safe and sound, Lord," she silently prayed.

"Sarah, you know what you mean to me." Cary gently put his hand under her chin and tilted her head up to look at him. "You know I've never had eyes for anyone else. I fell in love with you the first time I walked you home from school." Cary chuckled.

"What are you laughing at?" Sarah wanted to know.

"I'm not sure I should tell you," he said. Sarah had never been this close to Cary, face to face. She loved that dimple in his chin and his confident demeanor. His dark eyes looked full of mischief.

"You better tell me, Cary Evans! You can't go off and leave me wondering what you were thinking!"

"You were such a skinny little thing and you did look so sad after losing your mom. I wanted to take you in my arms and hug all the pain away. But I knew if I did, you'd never let me walk you home again."

"You've always seemed to understand me, Cary, and you're so right." Sarah could laugh a little at the memory. She never had figured out what Cary had seen in her before she blossomed into womanhood.

"Will you wait for me, Sarah? Do you want to be engaged to a man you might never see again?"

"Please don't talk like that. I can't imagine life with anyone but you, Cary." Sarah felt tears filling her eyes.

"Will you marry me, Sarah?" Cary's voice was barely above a whisper. Sarah could feel his breath against her hair.

She looked up at him and smiled her special smile that was just for him. "Yes, I will." For the first time their lips came together in a sweet, lingering promise. Time seemed to stand still as their hearts beat together as one.

Cary gently released her. His hands shook a little as he took a small box from his pocket. He opened it to reveal a diamond and ruby ring that sparkled in the darkening sky. "Oh, Cary, how did you manage to get a ring?" Sarah cried joyfully.

"I actually bought it the day before we heard the news of Pearl Harbor," Cary confessed. "I was beginning to worry that we wouldn't have a moment alone together before I had to leave."

"It's lovely. And the rubies make it perfect. You remembered how much I like my birthstone." Cary slid the ring onto Sarah's finger.

"Maybe we think we know everything about each other, Sarah, but I want us to spend a lifetime together finding out all there is to know." Then Cary took her hands and closed his eyes. "Dear God, we have pledged our love to one another and we ask You to bring us back together again. May this war be over soon."

They reluctantly parted and as Cary walked down the sidewalk, he turned and called back to her, "Until tomorrow."

As soon as Cary turned away, Sarah's waving hand stopped in mid-air and the tears she had controlled began to fall. "Until tomorrow," she heard herself say.

The next morning, Cary picked Sarah up and they continued to John's and then to Millie's. The four of them were exceptionally quiet as they drove toward the bus depot. No one thought to turn the radio on to hear Bing Crosby crooning his love songs. Each of them was thinking what they wanted to say in these last minutes.

As Cary turned into the parking lot the small-town bus depot was almost invisible -surrounded by the busses that the government had made available to transport the men to their camps. Men, women and children milled about not wanting to say goodbye. Many women were crying and others, like Sarah and Millie, tried to be brave. Snippets of countless farewells all blended together into one great cacophony. Each family unit seemed oblivious to the other families around them.

Sarah had a fleeting vision of Ava clinging to Howard as he passionately kissed her before the flow of the crowd came together again blocking her view. Cary embraced Sarah and reminded her of their prayers that God would keep him safe and bring them together again. John released Millie and the two men boarded the nearest bus.

As the busses began pulling away they reminded Sarah of caterpillars - the men's arms waving goodbye out the windows. Lovers called out last minute thoughts to one another but few could hear what was being said. The women and children and older men stood watching the busses go until they could no longer see them or hear their engines.

The noise of the busses was replaced by children just being children and their mothers telling them to come along. Sarah felt like she was dreaming. She turned and saw that Millie was walking by her side. Aunt Fan was just behind them with a stoic look on her face. Soon the parking lot and curbsides were empty. Everyone had returned to their homes to begin the quest to find a new normal.

Sarah tried to remember Cary's driving instructions as she chauffeured Millie and Aunt Fan through the clogged streets of Fair Pointe.

Chapter 12

A Letter

CHRISTMAS CAME. NO one felt like celebrating except the children. Pastor Redding and the other pastors in Fair Pointe made sure that the Christmas programs happened. As the reenactment of the Christmas story took place in Fair Pointe's churches, the smiling, happy faces of children playing their roles comforted the adults as much as it did the children. It was one of the sane things they still had to hang on to.

Weeks passed and ladies began to watch the mail for letters from their fiancés, husbands, sons and brothers. Sarah and Millie had found that going to work at the school and hearing the sounds of busy students each day helped them have peace of mind. Sarah also relied on her lifelong habit of retreating to the outdoors where she could hear and see God's beauty. Seeing God's creation soothed her like nothing else.

She and Cary had spent hours and hours exploring the great outdoors. Sometimes Sarah wished she could walk to work alone with her memories of Cary for company. But having Millie a block away was a blessing. When the January days were a bit too nippy, Sarah drove Cary's car and picked Millie up.

Aunt Fan handed Sarah the letter from Cary as soon as she arrived home from work one day in late January. It had been more than five weeks and the women of Fair Pointe were desperate for news of their loved ones.

Cary's letter read –

January 12, 1942

Dear Sarah whom I love with all my heart,

I am settling into this new life after surviving boot camp. I wish I could tell you where I am and exactly what I'm doing. I've learned so much and like the job they have assigned to me.

My daily routine begins at the crack of dawn. The days pass quickly and I sleep like a log every night. That's in spite of some of the men snoring.

I know by the time you receive this, Fair Pointe will be getting ready for all the colors of spring.

I wish I could be there with you but one day I will be and that's what we're looking forward to.

How are Aunt Fan and Millie and Ava? And everybody we know? John and I got to be together through boot camp and then he was sent in a different direction.

How are the Fair Pointe Panthers doing in their basketball season? Oh the fun we used to have at those games. You were always there to cheer me on and I know you're cheering me on now in the much bigger game of life and war. I feel your prayers all around me.

Your loving husband-to-be,
Cary

Just then Millie showed up, "Hello!" as she opened the front door coming in from the porch. She and Sarah were both holding up their letters with big grins. "Oh, it's so good to know John's all right," cried Millie.

They each read their letters out loud and all three ladies hung on every word, hearing John's voice and then Cary's. Letters would be their lifeline for the weeks and months ahead.

"Come on," said Millie, "let's go in the kitchen and write back to them right now!"

Aunt Fan set two plates of food down in front of the girls. They wrote and took bites and laughed and had to read parts of their letters to each other.

"Oh no!" cried Sarah. "We only have thirty minutes before we need to be at the auxiliary club. I don't want to miss it. I feel like I'm doing more for Cary if my hands are busy making something for him."

"Me, too," agreed Millie. "One nice thing about working for the high school is that it gives us some interesting stories to pass on to the guys."

Sarah added, "Cary will love to hear about Jimmy Adams scoring 37 points in the basketball game against the Foley Bears last Friday."

"And I need to tell John that Mr. Whiting's accounting tests are still to be feared as much as ever," laughed Millie. "Of course, my intelligent fiancé always managed to get an A."

On their way to the women's meeting Millie commented, "You know since our guys most likely are in the Pacific Theater I think our letters have a better chance of . . ." Millie stopped talking as soon as she realized what she was saying. She and Sarah had heard about the ships being sunk in the Atlantic. Not only were so many lives lost but thousands of letters to soldiers would never reach them.

Sarah knew Millie regretted her words. She pulled up in front of Doris's and said, "Come on, we're just on time."

Chapter 13

April Showers

"WELL, AUNTIE, THIS is the month when you will become a great aunt and I will become an aunt for the first time," commented Sarah. She loved Saturday mornings when she could leisurely eat her breakfast and enjoy a cup of coffee with her aunt. The front porch was once again decorated with Fan's plants and flowerpots. It had become their favorite place to enjoy a morning repast.

The latest news about the war drifted out from the living room but Sarah and Fan weren't attuned to it just then. "Yes, I was thinking about that this morning. In about a week we'll know if it's a boy or a girl.

"What a time to be born," went on Aunt Fan. "The poor little one won't even get to meet his father for who knows how long."

"Oh," Sarah said, "There's Howard's car pulling up right now." Aunt Fan and Sarah watched Ava pull herself out of the driver's side. Ava waddled up to the porch like a duck. Sarah wanted to laugh at her carefree sister being so encumbered that she could hardly walk but thought better of it.

"Good morning, dear," greeted Aunt Fan. "I still have some pancakes out if you would like to have a couple," she offered.

"No thank you, Aunt Fan. I had a bite to eat at home and I feel like I can't fit one more morsel of food into this stomach."

Ava eased herself down into one of the cushioned white rockers and sighed.

"It won't be long now, Sis, and you will be getting back to your normal size and have a little one to keep you company," comforted Sarah.

"Mom Hamlin had me baking bread with her all day yesterday. She wants us to have some extra food on hand for when the baby comes. Oh, I hope I don't have to do anymore baking," moaned Ava.

Sarah was glad to hear that Ava was cooperating with her mother-in-law. *Mrs. Hamlin really seems to have a way with my sister.*

"You two will be at the hospital with me, won't you?" asked Ava.

"We are planning on it," replied Sarah. "If you have the baby while I'm at work, I will come as soon as I get off and Aunt Fan will be with you. Of course, Mrs. Hamlin will be there, also, right?"

"Oh, she wouldn't miss it for anything," said Ava. She got a little smile on her face as she continued, "She is so excited to become a grandma. She helped me get the nursery all ready. That was finished a month ago but Mom keeps thinking of more items to collect. Ava looked apologetically at Aunt Fan and explained, "Mrs. Hamlin asked me to call her mom, I hope you don't mind, Auntie."

"Well of course I don't mind," replied Fan in her most practical voice.

"We heard from Howard a couple days ago. I have no idea where he is but at least I know that he's safe," said Ava.

Sarah and Millie had each received second letters from Cary and John. It took weeks for the letters to pass back and forth especially with the new V-mail method the government had begun. The letters had to pass through a postal censorship station before they were sent on to the families.

"I suppose you girls have heard about the rationing that we have to do. We will only be allowed certain amounts of food.

We will be issued a "War Ration Book," to keep track of what we purchase. I think I better buy some extra sugar because it will probably be one of the items rationed soon." Aunt Fan looked very preoccupied as she made a mental note.

"I hope Mom Hamlin bakes up some extra goodies to keep us in the sweets," added Ava, "and I hope she gets inspired to do it by herself!"

After Ava left and Sarah walked to Millie's, Aunt Fan went inside and knelt at her bed. "Dear Lord, please watch over my girls. Please help Ava not to have too hard a time when the little one comes. Please keep Cary and all our young men safe.

"And Lord, you know that Sarah wants to be reunited with her father. That's asking a lot, Lord, but you can change even Floyd."

Just last night, Sarah had brought up the subject of Floyd again. It was so hard for Aunt Fan to know how to encourage her at those times. What could she tell her? There were no promises that she could make.

Chapter 14

Two Years Later

"WILL THIS WAR never end?" demanded Ava. "I thought Howard would be back long before this. I can't believe that Julia is already two years old and hasn't met her dad." Ava and Julia had just finished lunch with the Hamlins.

Grandma Hamlin looked so sad. She worried more at night now, knowing that the longer the war continued, the more likely it was that they would receive bad news about their son. The gold star hung in the windows of many residents of Fair Pointe. Some of those mothers were good friends of Virginia's.

The ladies got up to clear the dishes from the table. "Grandma!" said little Julia. Mrs. Hamlin looked down at her granddaughter tugging at her apron. Her hazel eyes were bright with joy and her soft brown curls careened wildly in all directions. Julia had not a care in the world. She loved to come see the moo cows at Grandpa and Grandma's dairy farm. "Can we go see the cows?" pleaded Julia.

Ava looked at her adorable little daughter. Julia's world was a simple and happy one and Ava wanted to keep it that way. "Of course, we're going to see the cows! Are you coming to the pasture with us Grandma?" asked Ava.

"No, dear, not this time. I think I'll go lie down for a little while."

"But Grandma, it's not nap time yet," said Julia.

Mrs. Hamlin laughed and looked at Ava. "That little one is too precocious," she said.

"Well, today I'm going down for a nap before you, Julia. That just means you are getting to be a big girl now, honey."

Ava and Julia went out through the back door and walked hand in hand through the yard toward the pasture. Grandpa Hamlin got up from the table where they'd had lunch and chuckled as he watched them through the back window. "Those curls of hers have a mind of their own, don't they dear?"

They smiled at each other as they so often did when Ava and Julia came to see them. Julia's happy nature was contagious.

Ava and Julia were enjoying their walk through the tunnel of oak trees that lined the grassy road to the pasture. "Mommy, are the cows worried?" asked Julia. They'd never heard such mooing before.

"Let's go see what has them so upset." Ava reached down and swung Julia up into her arms.

When they got there, Geoff, one of the hired cow handlers, was on his horse herding the cows away from the pond. The two black and white border collies, Salt and Pepper, were doing a fantastic job of rounding the cattle up. Ava set Julia on top of the fence rail while they watched Geoff and the dogs herd the cattle toward the barn. Julia squealed in delight.

Geoff turned toward the sound and tipped his hat toward them. Ava wondered why Geoff would be bringing the cows back to the barn this early. Once the cows were well on their way Geoff directed his horse over to Ava.

"Good afternoon, lovely ladies," Geoff called to them. Ava smiled back at Geoff. She missed being made over and liked getting attention from the hired hand.

"Why are the cows being brought in so early?" asked Ava.

"Well, we've got some excitement going on in the pond," replied Geoff. "An eight-foot gator decided to take up residence there. I'm not too worried about the big cows but the calves might look like a tasty meal to that critter."

Julia was staring with fascination at Geoff while he talked. She loved seeing his cowboy hat and the big fancy saddle. "Can I ride Sarge with you, Joff?" Julia asked with her brightest smile. Her curls bounced as she tilted her head from side to side.

Geoff could never say no to Julia, "If it's okay with your mommy, little miss, it's okay with me. And I know it'll be okay with Sargent, right fella?" Geoff said as he patted the horse's neck. To Ava he said, "I have to get back to the house and call for some reinforcements to help me with this problem anyhow, so she can ride there with me if you want her to.

"I don't think that gator is planning to go anywhere but would you mind keeping an eye on him till I get back?" he asked Ava. "If we lose track of him now, he'll be hard to find."

"Oh, of course," responded Ava. She held Julia up on the fence rail till Geoff swept her onto the saddle in front of him. "Hang on, sweetheart!" admonished Ava.

Ava didn't have to wait long before she heard the neighboring farmers pull in with their pick-ups. Ava wondered if they planned to shoot the alligator.

Geoff was fairly new to the area so the men were explaining to him that Alabama had started protecting the alligators a few years ago and people could only kill them during hunting season. Since it wasn't hunting season, they would have to sedate the monster and move him to the farthest swamp.

Geoff rode over to Ava and thanked her for standing guard. "Julia got sleepy so Mr. Hamlin carried her into the house for a nap," he explained.

"Perfect, thanks," smiled Ava. Geoff looked down at her in a way that made her heart flutter a little. Then he tipped his hat and rode toward the men. Ava felt her heart pound in her chest as she watched him ride away.

"Let's hope this sedation dart penetrates," said the vet. Ava was fascinated watching the vet approach the pond with his dart gun ready. One of the neighbors, Mr. Nolan, had a skinned chicken on the end of a rope attached to a long pole to get the gator to expose his underside. He was in the back of a pick-up near where the gator was sunning. Mr. Nolan flung the bait in front of the gator to tempt him. Then he held the chicken up higher as the gator came toward it. The instant the alligator raised up to grab the chicken the crack of the dart gun sounded. The dart sunk into its soft underbelly. The huge creature swung its tail violently, splashing side to side for a few seconds before going still.

"Okay, men, let's do this fast," said the vet. "The anesthesia will wear off in about two hours."

Six men waded into the pond and lifted the heavy reptile into the back of Mr. Hamlin's pick-up.

Ava watched the entourage drive away as she walked through the oak trees back toward the barn. Matthew, the other hired man, came limping around the side of the barn as she approached. "Good afternoon, Matthew," said Ava.

"Quite the excitement, Mam!" greeted Matthew. "I guess the cows won't mind an earlier milking today," he explained.

Ava watched Matthew continue limping into the barn. She knew that his limp due to an injury in childhood had kept him from going to the battlefield. What a strange blessing, she thought.

Then her thoughts turned to Geoff. What was his story, she wondered? They knew next to nothing about him. He'd showed up a few weeks ago needing work and Mr. Hamlin was desperate for help and hired him on.

Chapter 15

Church Activities

ON A WARM Friday evening, Sarah and Millie walked through the neighborhoods to choir practice. Sarah told Millie all about the exciting adventure at the Hamlins'. Ava had stopped by with Julia the night before to tell Sarah and Aunt Fan all about it.

"Julia is such a hoot," said Sarah. "She helped her mom tell us all about the big alligator. Children sure are the spice of life, aren't they? Their innocent joy is contagious."

"Yeah, you should hear some of the things the five-year-olds say in Sunday school," replied Millie. "Last Sunday, the lesson was on Jonah and the whale. Bobby listened very attentively and then spoke up and said, 'I'm going to pray that God will send a whale to bring my daddy home. He's in a big ocean and sometimes the waves are so high just like the storm Jonah was in.'"

The friends chuckled a little but it also seemed sad at the same time. "If only we all could have that childlike faith," commented Sarah. "Sometimes it's hard for me to even picture Cary's face. We haven't seen one another for two and a half years."

"I know. I keep John's picture in front of me when I'm writing to him and that helps," replied Millie.

"You know where the picture of Cary is in my room," responded Sarah, "but a still photo of such a vibrant person doesn't help very much."

"Not to change the subject, but I don't know how long I will stay in the choir," Sarah confided. Millie had a feeling she knew what Sarah was going to say. "After Mrs. McGillivray said in front of everyone how beautifully I'd sung two Sundays ago, I heard a couple of the ladies making some snide comments when they thought I wasn't around. Then one of them came over to me and asked if we could talk. She told me that she didn't think my gift was singing."

"What!!!" cried Millie, "You have a beautiful voice! Well, of all the nerve, she had no right to say that."

"You know how much I dislike confrontations, Millie."

"I thought there might be some repercussions after Mrs. McGillivray complimented you," Millie acknowledged. "Sarah, you can't let what jealous ladies say keep you from using the talents God gave you. You know every church has its jealous cats and gossips," Millie stated matter-of-factly. "And it isn't just your voice they're jealous of. Who wants to stand next to a woman that looks like a movie star and then listen to her husband talk about how beautifully she sang or how nice she looked? You know what I mean. Men can be so ignorant of a woman's feelings."

"How do you know so much about this, Millie?" Sarah wanted to know. "After all you're not even married yet."

"I have parents and I've heard some of my dad's comments over the years. That's when my mom who's not exactly Miss America rolls her eyes. Then she's somewhat distant from Dad until she gets over it. You'd think he'd learn, right?

"And I've actually seen my mom snub the ladies that Dad has complimented. I hope John won't do that to me," Millie said. "And actually, I don't think Mom should treat those women any differently. It's not their fault if some man doesn't know enough to keep his mouth closed."

By now Sarah was laughing out loud at her friend. "Millie, we need to get you a soapbox to stand on and have all the married people at church come listen to your words of wisdom.

"Well, in any case, I know I need to forgive the ladies who aren't kind," Sarah said.

"Don't give them a second thought," advised Millie. "I overheard Mrs. Fields tell the beautiful Mrs. Jones that she wished she could look like her, at least for a day. And you're just as pretty as Mrs. Jones."

Sarah was still laughing, "Oh Millie, you are such a good friend and I know I should take your advice, although I have been thinking about working in the nursery instead of singing in the choir. Julia is in there and I'd like to spend more time with her. Children aren't complicated."

The two friends had arrived at the neighborhood church and entered the side door feeling that they had made some progress solving a few of life's problems.

Chapter 16

The Evans' Orchard

THE NEXT DAY, Sarah was at the Evans' pecan orchard for her twice a month visit with Cary's parents. Building her relationship with Cary's parents while he was gone had become one of the highlights of her life. Cary's older sister, Jean, joined them sometimes. She lived in Mobile and her husband was also away fighting.

Jean got them all caught up on the latest gossip at the shipbuilding plant. "These husbands better get back soon," said Jean. "I think the assembly line manager thinks he's the ladies' man of the year. He seems to be enjoying his position over those young ladies a bit too much if you ask me. Then he comes into my office and asks my advice when it all gets to be too much for him," finished Jean.

"What's the world coming to?" asked Mrs. Evans. "I can't even imagine that many women all working together in one place for ten hours a day - and doing men's jobs to boot!"

"Well, Mom, I kid you not; some of those women do a better job than the men."

"I know it has to be this way for the war," replied Mrs. Evans, "but I hope when things get back to normal everyone will remember how important it is to raise the next generation."

"And don't forget, Jo Ann," added Mr. Evans, "I've told you many times how much I appreciate the way you keep our home clean and cozy. My mom had to work to support us kids and the lack of time she had to do the housekeeping really made it less of a home."

"I know, dear, and thank you," agreed Mrs. Evans. "Jean, why don't you two girls look at some of the photo albums while I wash the dishes." Sarah, you'll find some pictures that you are in, at least from the year 1935." She suddenly realized that was the year that Sarah's mother had died and wished she hadn't mentioned it.

But the two young ladies were already pulling an album out of the hutch. Sarah seemed not to have noticed. A lot of healing can happen in nine years, thought Mrs. Evans.

Soon she heard the girls laughing and her curiosity got the better of her. "What's so funny?" she asked as she entered the living room. Mr. Evans had peaked over their shoulders and he was laughing as well.

"Oh Mom, this was the summer that you gave me a camera for my birthday," laughed Jean. "I took it everywhere with me. Here I got a picture of Sarah telling Cary off after he rescued her from drowning, at least he thought she was drowning. Sarah and Betty had advanced to the lifeguard class. Sarah was supposed to pretend she was drowning and one of the other students would jump in and save her. Well, Cary and his friend, Rob, showed up just in time to hear Sarah calling for help and going under. Cary, with his natural enthusiasm dove into the pool immediately to save her.

"It was so funny," Jean was laughing so hard she couldn't continue.

"So as Cary's trying to get his arm around my neck to save me, Betty is behind him trying to pull him away and explain that she's supposed to save me. Well, you know how determined Cary can be. So I finally gave up and let him drag me to the side and lift me out of the pool," giggled Sarah. "But Betty never did give up and was hitting Cary all the way to the side. He tried to fend her off but he had to keep a good hold of me as well." By now all four of them were laughing.

"Of course, I had my camera and got a shot of them after the rescue. Look at how mad Sarah looks, and Cary looks so embarrassed. Good thing you were being so vocal, Sarah, or Cary might have tried to resuscitate you. I had to hide this picture from him that summer because he threatened to tear it to shreds." They all agreed that it felt so good to reminisce over the good old days for a while.

"You know, Sarah, it always did amaze me that Cary seemed to consider himself to be your appointed guardian," observed Jo Ann.

"Yes, it took me a while to learn to appreciate it," explained Sarah, "but he won my friendship that first year. And then, well, you all know the rest of the story . . ."

Jean suddenly got quiet. She wasn't about to admit how jealous she had been of Sarah at first when she saw how nicely her brother treated her. It had taken Jean a while to warm up to Sarah.

After they'd had their dessert and coffee, Bob Evans walked out to the mailbox. He held a letter from Cary when he came back.

"Let's read it together, shall we?" he offered.

Dear Dad and Mom,

I want to thank you for teaching me to work hard. Growing up working in our pecan orchard really prepared me for this rigorous life in a hot climate.

Most of the time I'm inside but I can't tell you about that.

I'm doing fine and feel pretty good most of the time. I miss you both and Sarah and Jean very much. I miss Fair Pointe and all the fun we always had. But we've all had to grow up.

I like to go to the outdoor church service on the deck when we can. The pastor gives good messages just like Pastor Redding.

Things are going well. Maybe I'll be back home by Christmas.

I hope you'll have enough help with the pecans this summer, Dad.

Keep praying we won't have to go through anymore storms. It didn't seem like we could make it but God had his hand over us.

I can't wait to get back and for Sarah and me to begin our life together.

Your loving son,
Cary

"How terrible it must be on board a ship in a bad storm. His last letter said the ship was nearly on its side in the worst of the storm," Jo Ann fretted.

"I know," responded Sarah. That was just one more thing she didn't want to think about. There were enough worries without thinking about storms that no one can control.

Jean said she needed to get back to Mobile. Sarah wanted to walk through the pecan orchard before leaving. It gave her a feeling of peace to walk where Cary had spent so many hours working alongside his dad. Sarah laughed a little while she walked through the orchard, remembering some of the pictures they'd seen that afternoon. She and Cary had so many great memories together. "Oh, Lord, it feels so good to laugh a little again. Please may this war end soon," Sarah pleaded.

Chapter 17

Mobile

SARAH HOPPED INTO Cary's car and drove to Millie's. Millie was waiting and came out as soon as Sarah pulled into their driveway. Summer holiday meant that they only did work at the school as was needed. It usually amounted to about three days a week. So the girls were thinking of fun things to do on their extra days off.

"It feels like vacation, doesn't it, Millie?" Sarah said gleefully.

"Yes, and we are ready to have some fun!" Millie laughed. "Even though we don't get to drive much with the gasoline rationing, it sure is nice that Cary left his car with you."

Sarah nodded and headed toward the highway to Mobile. They passed small, tidy farms with pecan orchards and cows grazing in pastures. "I think we must live in the most beautiful place in the world," Sarah commented.

Soon they were passing through the quaint streets of Daphne. "Don't you just love driving through these canopies of oak trees?" asked Millie

The girls came to the highway and headed west toward Mobile. The causeway afforded wonderful views of the Mobile Bay. "Seeing the sun reflecting on the water reminds me of Julia's latest saying. Whenever she sees the sun reflecting off the pond, she calls it 'shine-shine.'"

Millie smiled benevolently and truly understood her friend's adoration of the charming little girl.

"Oh, I better slow down, Millie, that truck is apparently stalled," Sarah noticed as they sped along. A large semi-truck had pulled onto the shoulder. The driver was waving to them to stop.

Sarah pulled in behind the truck and the driver approached Millie's side of the car. As he got closer both girls turned and looked at each other. It was Thomas whom they hadn't seen since Ava's wedding.

Millie had her window down and Thomas bent down and grinned at the girls. "Well, I don't believe my eyes," he joked. "I sure didn't expect to see you two out here. Where are you headed?"

Sarah explained that they were going to Mobile for the day. "Is everything okay?" she asked.

"Actually, no, my truck has a blown tire and unfortunately someone didn't put a spare in the storage compartment. I'll have to go into Mobile to get one and hope they have a couple. Do you girls mind if I ride along to Mobile with you?"

"Of course not," answered Sarah. "I seem to remember you telling me that your dad's company would be hauling metal for the war effort. So I'll just consider this my contribution." Sarah smiled at Thomas as he hopped into the backseat.

The three of them continued on to Mobile and got caught up on what they'd all been doing. The smell of salt water blew in through the open windows of the car. They all had to raise their voices to be heard above the sound of rushing air.

A man stood by the side of the road ahead with his thumb out. "Should I pick up this hitchhiker?" asked Sarah.

"Sure," both Millie and Thomas agreed. "There are quite a few who get around that way now thanks to the gas rationing," said Thomas.

Sarah pulled over and the middle-aged man got in the back next to Thomas. "I sure do thank you for stopping," said the gentleman.

"We're happy to help," said Sarah. "Where are you headed?"

"You can just let me off at the harbor in Mobile. I'm going to the Gulf Shipbuilding plant for the afternoon shift," the man explained.

It felt good to Sarah to be driving along with three people in the car. It almost felt festive as they all continued talking and laughing. Before she knew it, the man was getting out of the car at the port. "Goodbye, and take care, sir," she called out her window. He waved and smiled.

"Now where do we take you, Thomas?" asked Millie.

He directed Sarah to the tire shop and was about to get out to go in when he stopped and looked back at Sarah. "I don't want to horn in on your plans, but how about the three of us get a bite to eat together after I get my tire? Then I'll hitchhike back to where my truck is."

Sarah and Millie looked at each other and knew they both liked his idea. "That would be nice," said Sarah. "We'll wait here for you."

"Sarah, can you believe this?" asked Millie. "What are the chances? Do you think Cary will mind if we have lunch with Thomas?"

"I don't know, Millie. All the time that's passed without seeing Cary and the long periods of time between letters has dulled my memories of him," Sarah said with a sad look.

"You always said he wasn't the jealous type, so maybe he wouldn't mind. He would want you to have some fun I guess."

"I guess so, Millie. But help me remember that I'm a woman who's engaged to a man who's fighting so you and I can live in freedom. And I love Cary. It's just that sometimes it seems impossible that he'll survive and come back."

"Here comes Thomas," warned Millie.

"Okay, we already told him yes, so let's forget the problems for now and keep enjoying our day trip," suggested Sarah.

Millie gave a thumbs-up as Thomas opened the trunk and put his two tires in.

"Okay, ladies, I'm just along for the ride, so wherever you want to go will be fine with me."

"We were going to walk around downtown and choose a place," explained Sarah.

"I come through Mobile quite a lot," replied Thomas, "so if you want my opinion, I'd be happy to help."

"Sure," both girls called in unison.

Thomas guided Sarah to Hattie's, a quaint, family-run restaurant that he said served meals like you'd get at home.

When they entered the café, Thomas seemed to know the hostess and the waitresses. Sarah noticed how they all hung on his every word and gave him their biggest smiles. She and Millie kept looking at each other surreptitiously as they noticed what a flirt Thomas was. It came so naturally to him, Sarah doubted that he was even aware of it. She thought about Cary and how he acted in a group of mostly women. He was friendly but it was much more of a brotherly friendliness, like the way Cary treated his sister.

Once they had placed their orders, Thomas turned his full attention on Sarah and Millie. He had a way of getting people to open up and talk about themselves. Sarah remembered that trait from when she first met him in Tallahassee.

Soon the three of them were laughing and talking like lifelong friends. Sarah couldn't remember the last time she'd had so much fun.

As they walked out the door Sarah turned just in time to see the cute blond waitress give Thomas a coy wink. Sarah couldn't see his face but the waitress seemed undeterred.

Thomas assured the girls that he'd have no trouble getting a ride back to the truck since hitchhiking had become a common mode of transportation in the United States.

After they let Thomas off, Millie suggested they go back and walk along the harbor and then do a little window shopping at the adjacent shops downtown.

They kept finding themselves talking about Thomas. "That guy is a lady magnet," observed Millie.

Sarah agreed that Thomas was a regular flirt and the women seemed drawn to him.

"I feel sorry for whoever he marries," Millie began philosophizing. "She will always feel like she's competing for his attention."

"I wonder if he has girlfriends in all the towns that he drives his truck to," Sarah speculated.

Millie's answering expression said it all.

Chapter 18

New Developments

"ARE YOU SURE you won't mind having Julia and me right under your noses, Mom and Dad Hamlin?" Ava inquired. "I know how you adore Julia but having us around all the time might get to be too much."

"It's not as though you'll be in the house with us, honey," encouraged Virginia. "You and Julia can have your privacy in the extra cabin we have available. But, you're right about saving up some money for when Howard returns. That's a very good idea."

"Okay, I'll let Mr. Weiss know that we'll be moving out."

"I'll come over tomorrow and help you pack up your things," volunteered Virginia. "Oh, it will be so much fun having you two nearby."

"I'll see if Geoff or Matthew will help us get you moved," Mr. Hamlin said as he headed out the door.

"Thanks Dad and Mom," said Ava. It was a new experience for her to have two people in her life that treated her like a daughter.

The weeks were flying by as Ava and Julia were settling into the cabin at the Hamlins' place. Julia loved seeing the cows and "Joff's" horse every day.

"Julia, would you like to go see Granny and Aunt Sarah today?" Ava asked her daughter. Julia had started calling Great Aunt Fan, "Granny," and it had stuck.

"Oh, yes! Mommy, I love to go to Granny's," Julia answered.

When Ava and Julia entered the back door into the kitchen, Sarah was washing the breakfast dishes and handing them to Fan who stood by with a dish towel.

"How's the hired-hand's cabin?" inquired Aunt Fan.

"It's perfect for the two of us," said Ava. "When Howard gets back, the men will have to get busy and build us the house we'd talked about before the war started."

Sarah picked Julia up and gave her a big hug. "How's my favorite person in the whole world?"

Julia giggled and snuggled in closer to Sarah's neck. "Does this angelic child of yours ever get unhappy about anything?" she asked her sister.

"Oh, trust me; she has her moments just like every other two-year-old, Sis. But she's good most of the time, that's for sure!" Ava winked at her daughter.

"Julia would you like a piece of Granny's banana bread?" asked Aunt Fan.

They sat at the kitchen table instead of the porch to avoid the summer heat. "Your banana bread is just as good as I remember it," Ava complimented Fan. Sarah set a cup of milk down in front of Julia and brewed a pot of tea for them to enjoy.

"Granny, where's Miss Betsy?" asked Julia.

"Your Miss Betsy is resting upstairs," Aunt Fan assured the little girl. "I'll go get her for you while Mommy cleans your face and hands."

Aunt Fan came back with Miss Betsy who liked to stay at Granny's. They congregated in the living room around the radio.

"I think it's all right to have the news on, don't you?" asked Fan. "Julia is occupied with Miss Betsy."

"Yes, that's fine," said Ava.

The ladies were excited to hear that the Japanese were getting beaten badly in the Pacific Theater. "I think Mr. Hamlin is right," said Ava, "that the war will end soon."

"It's important for us to have hope and keep praying," replied Fan.

"To change the subject," she continued, "Mrs. Buckley next door asked me if I'll be entering my roses in the competition at the fair this year. She's been trying to beat me for three years." Aunt Fan chuckled.

"Mom doesn't plan to enter her apple pie this year. She wants to try for first prize with her new triple-berry recipe. I think she'd take the prize no matter what kind of pie she makes," Ava said.

Julia was smoothing Miss Betsy's hair and jabbering away contentedly on Fan's braided rug.

On the way back to the dairy farm, Ava suddenly felt a jolt and the steering wheel pull to one side. She slowed the car down and pulled over to the side of the road. Julia had fallen asleep on the back seat.

An elderly man with a cane hobbled across his yard and called out to Ava, "Yep, you've got yourself a flat tire, Miss."

Ava got out and could see that she wouldn't get any farther with the deflated tire. "Would you mind if I use your phone?" she asked.

"Not a problem, young lady, come right this way. This is my wife, Mrs. Oglesby," the kind man said as they approached the front porch.

Ava smiled at her. "My daughter is asleep in the back seat. Would you mind keeping an eye on the car while I make the call?"

"I'd be happy to," said Mrs. Oglesby. Mr. Oglesby showed Ava inside.

"Help will be here soon," Ava explained when she came back out. She visited with the folks on their porch and kept an eye on the car where Julia was napping. Thankfully, the sun was headed down and a cool breeze was blowing from the bay.

Ava was surprised to see Geoff sitting behind the wheel of Mr. Hamlin's truck as it pulled in behind Howard's car. He got out and walked toward the car and opened the trunk. Geoff got the jack and tire iron out and soon had the flat tire removed. *The silent cowboy type,* thought Ava.

The sounds woke Julia. Ava pulled her out of the back seat so she could watch "Joff" change the tire. She wanted to know all about it. When Geoff was nearly finished Ava took Julia's hand and led her to the Oglesby's porch to thank them.

"You have a nice-looking husband, Ava," Mrs. Oglesby said. "He's a real handsome cowboy."

"Oh, Mrs. Oglesby, Geoff isn't my husband," explained Ava. "He's one of the hired hands at my in-laws' dairy farm. My husband is away fighting in the war."

"Oh, honey, I'm sorry," apologized Mrs. Oglesby.

Ava thanked them for helping her and walked back to her car where Geoff was waiting for her.

Geoff opened the door for her and Julia to get in. "How would you ladies like to have an ice cream cone?" he asked. "No reason why we can't stop at the Dairy Top on our way home."

Ava looked up at him and couldn't resist. She could use a fun outing. "Sounds like an excellent plan, Geoff. We'll follow you."

Julia was turning somersaults in the back seat. "Ice Cweem, oh good!"

The three of them sat on a bench next to the Dairy Top and enjoyed their cones. The mockingbirds were singing their evening song. Julia had chocolate ice cream all over her face and Geoff laughed as he got his napkin wet with water from his cup and wiped her face.

"This has been such a nice treat," Ava said. "Thank you for coming to our rescue and treating us." She looked at Geoff and hoped it was dark enough that he couldn't see the blush on her cheeks.

"My pleasure," Geoff replied. Then he carried Julia to Ava's car and opened the door for Ava. "See you back at the farm," Geoff called over his shoulder.

Ava gave a parting wave and drove away.

When the two vehicles pulled into the Hamlins' yard, both Mom and Dad Hamlin came hurrying out of the house. "We were getting worried," Virginia said.

"You were gone quite a while," added Mr. Hamlin.

Again, Ava was glad for the darkness as she felt herself blushing. "Well, Geoff treated us to ice cream cones," Ava replied. "I'm sorry you were worried."

"Oh, I see," was all Mr. Hamlin could think to say.

Suddenly things seemed awkward as they all parted to go to their homes.

"Night, night," called Julia from her mom's shoulder.

They blew Julia goodnight kisses from the lighted porch and watched them walk to their cabin.

Chapter 19

Temptations

AVA HELD JULIA in her arms as they waved goodbye to Grandpa and Grandma Hamlin. Their daughter, Nora, had called to ask if Virginia could please come to Dothan, Georgia to help out in their grocery store. The person who normally worked in the store alongside Nora had fallen and was laid up. It had been too long since Mrs. Hamlin had seen her daughter.

They decided Mr. Hamlin would take Virginia to Dothan. That way he could have a short visit with their daughter before coming back to the dairy farm. He knew that Geoff and Matthew would keep things running smoothly for a couple days while he was away.

Mrs. Hamlin was so excited that she would have some time with her daughter. It wouldn't be easy working long hours in the store and being on her feet that much, but she was willing to do it in order to spend time with Nora.

The next morning, Ava and Julia were sitting on the porch when Geoff came by on his horse, Sargent. With Salt and Pepper's help he'd gotten the cows back out to pasture after the morning milking.

"Salt! Pepper!" called Julia. "Come!" The black and white dogs loped over to get their pets and hugs from Julia. Geoff followed on Sargent.

Ava felt her heartbeat speed up as Geoff approached. "Would you like a cup of coffee?" she offered.

Geoff easily dismounted Sargent and let the reigns hang down so his horse could nibble on the grass. "That sounds good," he answered.

Ava disappeared inside and Geoff knelt next to Julia to reward Salt and Pepper with pats and words of praise. "Our dogs are the best cow dogs around, aren't they Julia?" His dark eyes shone into Julia's. His curly light brown hair was getting somewhat long. He'd have to get to the barber's soon.

"Your hair is like mine," Julia giggled.

Geoff winked at Julia and said, "You know, I think you're right."

Ava could hear Geoff's rich laughter as she brought two cups of coffee out of the cabin. She sat down and offered the other chair to Geoff. The view of the live oak trees and the green pasture where the cows grazed made for a very peaceful scene.

"So, tell me about yourself," invited Ava. "What brought you to Fair Pointe to work on a dairy farm?"

Geoff told her about growing up in a small farming community in Pennsylvania and how he'd learned to ride a horse at a young age. Ava noticed that he didn't seem to want to talk about his family except to say that he'd been close to his grandparents until they passed away when he was twelve.

"What about you, Ava?" Geoff questioned. "Have you always lived in Fair Pointe?" Geoff couldn't help but admire Ava's beauty and her mischievous eyes.

"My sister and I moved here from Longview, Texas, when I was ten years old. Our Aunt Fan was visiting. We went for a drive in my mom's new car and someone hit us from behind. Our car went off the road and tipped over. My mom was the only one who was seriously injured. She died several days later from an injury to her head." Ava wondered why she was telling Geoff so much about her life.

"I'm sorry," Geoff said gently. "That must have been very hard for you and Sarah. How old was Sarah then?"

"She was thirteen." Ava was afraid Geoff would ask about their dad next but he didn't. He seemed to sense that he should let Ava lead the conversation where she wanted it to go.

"Do you miss your parents?" Ava redirected the conversation back to Geoff.

"Oh, uh, my mom got sick and died a number of years ago and my dad is a businessman who lives overseas." Geoff seemed very uncomfortable so Ava didn't pursue the topic.

They both looked at Julia who was perched on the porch step. Sargent had his head down and was letting Julia pat his nose. "Animals seem to know how much Julia likes them," Ava said.

"That's for sure," replied Geoff. "They definitely sense her loving spirit."

"Mommy, I really want to ride Sarge," Julia looked hopefully at her mom and then at Geoff.

Geoff looked back at Ava with a question in his eyes. She smiled and laughed as she said, "Well, honey, that's up to Geoff. Maybe he has other things he has to do."

"I'm never too busy to entertain two lovely ladies. How about we saddle up Penny and the three of us go for a ride?" Geoff felt like he was holding his breath suggesting such a daring thing and waited to see if Ava would rebuff him.

The fact that he was extending the invitation when the Hamlins were out of town was a glaring thought in both his and Ava's mind. She tilted her head back and laughed again before saying, "I haven't been on a horse for so long; that sounds wonderful."

"Great!" smiled Geoff. "We can ride to the bay. I might even go for a swim."

"I'll pack a lunch for us," Ava acquiesced and turned to Julia, "Come on honey, let's make a picnic lunch to take on our fun outing." Julia was jumping up and down for joy unable to contain her excitement over the new developments.

"I'll get Penny saddled and be back," said Geoff. "Do you, um, want the side saddle?" Geoff looked at Ava's skirt as he spoke.

"Oh, no, I'd rather not. I'll change into my culottes."

When Geoff entered the barn, Matthew was brushing Penny. Geoff explained that he needed to get her bridled and saddled.

"I saw you and Ava talking," drawled Matthew. "And now the three of you are going riding together?"

"Come on, Matt," Geoff said, "It's just a horseback ride. Don't make it sound like we're up to no good."

"She's a very beautiful woman, isn't she?" asked Matthew.

Geoff gave him a dark look and took hold of Penny's harness. "You mind your business and I'll mind mine," Geoff said as he led Penny away.

"Have it your way," retorted Matthew.

Chapter 20

The Horseback Ride

AVA FELT LIKE a young girl again as she galloped through the trees with the wind in her hair. She realized she'd gotten too far ahead of Geoff and Julia. She pulled Penny up and turned to see that Geoff was being careful with his little rider seated in front of him.

Geoff looked as happy as Ava felt. They both sensed this was an unusual day that was meant to be enjoyed. Julia was full of comments about her first time to go so fast on Sarge. Ava had never seen her daughter look so thrilled.

Geoff wanted to show Ava the discovery he had made the week before. "Come on, I want to show you something I found."

Ava was intrigued and gently dug her heels into Penny's side to follow Sargent. "Come on, Mommy!" Julia cried.

Geoff led them through a jungle-like trail for half a mile. Suddenly they rounded a bend and entered a double-wide path through Azalea bushes. At the end of the flowery path, they came to an open space. In front of them was an old brick house in the middle of an overgrown yard. It had obviously sat empty for quite some time.

"Oh," Ava's voice was filled with awe. "I wonder who lived here and why they left."

"Sometime I'll show you the inside," said Geoff, "but the floor is pretty rough and it's not the best place for a two-year-old."

"I can do it," Julia informed them.

Geoff and Ava looked at each other and laughed. "I know you can, honey, but we better get to the beach and have our picnic. Maybe some other time we'll explore this old place."

"Ok," agreed Julia.

"Giddy-up," Geoff encouraged Sargent.

Behind the house was an old road that led down toward the bay with a creek running alongside it. The creek wound this way and that through the trees, sometimes bordering the dirt road.

"It's getting hot," said Geoff. "I'm glad I brought my swimming trunks. That water is going to feel mighty good."

Ava wondered where he'd change and felt herself blushing from more than the heat.

"Look Julia, do you see the water through the trees?" Geoff asked her. He directed her head in the right direction and waited for her to see ahead toward the shining gulf.

"Oh! Look Mommy, I see the shine-shine on the big water!"

Ava laughed and explained to Geoff that shine-shine meant sunshine.

Soon the trail brought them all the way down to where the trees ended. Julia yelped in sheer delight at the sight of sand and water as far as her eyes could see.

They picked a spot to dismount where the horses could stay in the shade of the trees. There were some stumps and a fallen tree to sit on next to the meandering creek. Ava took their lunch from the saddle bags and passed a sandwich to Geoff and half a sandwich to Julia.

Julia took a bite and carried her sandwich first one way and then another to see everything around them. The horses were drinking from the creek.

"This is a beautiful place, Geoff, thanks for bringing us here. I think there's a park just around the outcropping of land over there." Ava pointed toward it. "If it's the park I'm thinking of, Howard . . . um, we used to picnic there."

Geoff smiled at Ava and knew she felt awkward mentioning Howard's name. Julia had finished her half-sandwich and came over for the next course. Ava handed her an apple slice and Julia set off with it toward the creek and her pile of sticks she'd collected.

After lunch Julia was getting a little bored with her stick creations. Every time she thought she'd built something it collapsed. Ava noticed Julia's frustration. She turned to Geoff and whispered, "It's about nap time for her. I don't think she'll last much longer."

Geoff laid out his towel and told Ava that would make a good place for Julia to have her nap. "I'll be back," he said and mysteriously disappeared into the trees.

When Geoff came back he had changed into his swim trunks and Ava was gently stroking Julia's forehead as she lay on Geoff's towel. They kept quiet as they watched Julia's eyelids close and then open several times. Finally, she succumbed to sleep.

Ava looked up at Geoff and found him watching her intently. The air seemed alive with electric current. Ava felt an involuntary shiver run down her spine. Neither of them wanted to be the first one to speak. What was there to say? They both knew what was happening between them. The thing Ava didn't want to face was the fact that falling in love with Geoff was adultery.

She looked down at Julia. There in her daughter's face she saw something of the man she had given herself to, her first and only love. "Help me, God," Ava prayed. As soon as the words were out of her mouth Ava saw Howard's face. His eyes were soft and pleading, begging her not to give herself to another. Then a flash of blinding light came between them and his face disappeared from her sight.

Geoff couldn't imagine what thoughts were going through Ava's mind. He felt at loose ends not knowing what to do. He knew she had strong feelings for him so why was he afraid to touch her?

When Ava looked up at Geoff again, the strong pull she'd felt minutes before had waned. Geoff knew the moment had passed as well and got up.

"I guess I'm ready for that swim," he said. Ava watched Geoff jog toward the beach and felt a little breeze pass over her face. She felt tremendous relief as though she'd just been spared from a terrible accident. *But how much longer can I be around Geoff without succumbing to his charms?*

Chapter 21

Repercussions

MR. HAMLIN HAD returned home and things seemed somewhat normal again. Ava was carefully avoiding Geoff's company. She didn't trust her feelings and she didn't want her father-in-law to see the turmoil her heart was causing her. *Oh why does life have to be so complicated? What's wrong with an eighteen-year-old having a little entertainment?* Ava argued with her conscience. She knew she'd made the right decision at the beach the other day, but seeing Geoff always stirred feelings in her.

"I love you, Mommy," Julia seemed to have a sixth sense about people when they were having a difficult time.

Ava looked at her daughter and forgot about herself for a minute. "Mommy, can Joff be my daddy?" asked Julia.

Ava looked at Julia's innocent little face surrounded by the unruly curls. The question startled her. "Julia, you little monkey." Ava couldn't help laughing in spite of herself. "How do you do it?"

Julia had no idea what her mom meant but she was relieved to see her mommy laughing. When they finished their little interlude of giggling, Ava said, "No, honey, Geoff isn't your dad. Your daddy is away fighting some very bad men. Ava walked over to the little hutch and picked up Howard's letters. "He writes to us, honey. Listen, in this letter, he asks, 'How's my little Julia?'"

That made Julia smile. "Will he come back to see us?" asked Julia.

What can I tell her? What if I say yes and he doesn't come back? And I can't tell her he may not come back. That's too much for her little mind to deal with.

Julia was patiently waiting for the answer. Her trusting hazel eyes were looking at Ava. In desperation, Ava said what she'd always heard Aunt Fan say, "God will take care of us. We just have to trust him." Then she added, "Your daddy wants to come back to us as soon as he can."

Julia solemnly nodded her head. Ava wondered how she'd gotten such a perceptive little girl.

Just then there was a knock on the door and Ava walked across the room and opened the door. "Grandpa Hamlin!" cried Julia joyfully. She ran to him and he picked her up giving her a big hug.

"Good morning, sunshine," he said. They kissed each other's cheeks.

"Ava, I'd like to talk with you," said Mr. Hamlin. "Can Julia play in the yard while we visit on the patio?"

Ava felt a foreboding inside. She was puzzled about what Dad Hamlin would want to talk to her about. She was pretty sure she'd kept her feelings for Geoff well hidden.

Julia's little legs carried her quickly across the yard to the castle Grandpa had built for her. Her swing hung from the branch of an oak tree nearby.

Mr. Hamlin and Ava walked to the patio and sat down. Ava looked at him nervously. The way he looked at her just then reminded her of Aunt Fan's talks. Whenever Ava was headed for disaster, Aunt Fan had a talk with her.

"This is uncomfortable for me, Ava, but a couple people have informed me that you and Geoff have been doing things together. I got a call this morning from someone who saw the three of you at the Dairy Top and . . . well, I heard about the horseback ride."

Mr. Hamlin didn't want to get Matthew in trouble. "People think you're being disloyal to Howard, you see . . ."

"I'm only eighteen, Dad. Do you really expect me to never get together with other young people to have a little fun?" asked Ava. "Let the old gossips say whatever they want," Ava argued.

"Ava, you can get together with other people your age, but it's not wise to go alone with a young man. I know Geoff is lonely and he finds you very attractive and I know you get lonely. Howard's been gone for a long time." Mr. Hamlin suddenly sighed and put his head down. "The two of you getting together is like a ticking bomb. Please, Ava, try to understand. I know you're young but the choices we make in our youth last for the rest of our lives."

"Who would I get together with, Dad?" Ava looked up at him and continued, "I don't have any girlfriends."

Mr. Hamlin looked thoughtful before saying, "Why don't you talk to Sarah and tell her you'd like to go with her and Millie sometimes. When Virginia gets back, she and I can watch Julia so you can have a break now and then."

Ava smiled at him noncommittally, just as she'd smiled at Aunt Fan so many times. Somehow when people tried to direct her life, Ava felt compelled to resist. "Why was that?" she wondered. Julia wasn't like that. She almost always wanted to please the people she loved.

Mr. Hamlin watched Ava and felt at a loss. He'd tried and that's all he knew to do. Maybe it was time to look into Geoff's background and find out where he'd come from. But if Geoff leaves, who would replace him?

Chapter 22

News

SARAH ARRIVED HOME from a day at work in mid-June and found Aunt Fan crying. "Aunt Fan! What's wrong?" cried Sarah as she knelt in front of her. It wasn't like Aunt Fan to cry over anything trivial. This had to be something big. Thoughts raced through Sarah's mind.

Aunt Fan looked up at Sarah and looked so despairing that Sarah felt more worried for her aunt than for what she was about to hear.

"Sarah, I received some very bad news this afternoon," began Aunt Fan. Fan paused and looked at Sarah as if she couldn't go on. Sarah took Fan's hand and slowly nodded for her to continue.

Fan knew her next words would change everything in Sarah's life instantly. She prayed silently for God to give Sarah strength. "Jo Ann Evans called me." The color drained out of Sarah's face.

Fan faltered and tears fell down her cheeks. "Cary's ship was torpedoed on May 29."

Sarah couldn't think of any words to say. Time seemed to have stopped. Aunt Fan's face looked far away, like she was seeing it through one of the pipes she and Cary had used for their spyglasses. Fan's lips were moving.

Sarah willed herself back to reality. Her Aunt's voice sounded flat, "The ship was sunk and only a few were rescued. Cary wasn't among them."

Sarah sank back onto the floor in stunned silence. The thing she'd been dreading for two and a half years had happened. She couldn't take it in. She thought about Doris and Betty and others she knew who had the Gold Star flags hanging in their windows.

Sarah put her head down in Aunt Fan's lap as the tears began to fall.

How much time passed, Sarah didn't know. Aunt Fan was gently stroking her hair. Sarah realized that she had to go to the Evans'. "Aunt Fan, will you come with me to the Evans'?"

"If it will make it easier for you, of course I will come," Aunt Fan replied.

The two of them arrived at the Evans' farm just before the sun set. The Evans held out their arms to Sarah as she and Aunt Fan entered. The three of them stood with their arms around each other and cried. Aunt Fan sat nearby with a tissue to her nose.

When they recovered enough to talk, Mrs. Evans told them how the Western Union courier had come to their door. As soon as she'd seen him, she knew there was horrendous news they would all have to bear.

"His body was never found," said Jo Ann. "Many of the bodies were recovered, but most were not."

"Listen," said Mr. Evans softly, "Cary's life has always been in God's hands. If he is dead, then he's in heaven with the Lord."

"What do you mean, Bob? Is it possible that he could have survived and wasn't found?"

"I'm not saying that, Jo Ann. But when there's no body, how can we not hope that he may have survived?"

The four of them sat quietly with thoughts swirling in their heads.

Finally, Jo Ann spoke, "I'd rather know for certain. I can't live wondering if my son is still alive somewhere, wondering what happened to him."

"We must leave it in God's hands and ask Him to help us get through this." Mr. Evans looked at each of them. "Cary knew you both to be strong women. He would want us to face this bravely and together. When a man goes to war, he absolutely knows he may never return."

Chapter 23

Sarah Doubts

ALONE IN HER room that night, Sarah lay awake thinking. Tomorrow she would have to tell Millie. She had been too emotionally worn out to go there after she and Aunt Fan returned home.

Aunt Fan told Sarah she would call the Hamlins and ask them to talk to Ava and to tell her that Sarah had gone to bed and needed to rest.

Sarah was exhausted but sleep wouldn't come. Instead her mind played scenes of her and Cary together. The reel of memories played over and over again in her head. Even with her heart broken into pieces, Sarah had to laugh when the comical scenes scrolled past her mind's eye. She relived the pool rescue and caught herself laughing hysterically. Then the brutal truth assaulted her once again. Sarah rolled onto her side and wept into her pillow.

The mental wrestling continued all night. It was far worse than any nightmare she'd ever had, even when her mother had died. How could Cary be gone? He'd been her best friend ever since he'd seen her at school after Aunt Fan had brought them back to Fair Pointe to live with her. They'd done a thousand things together – swimming in the bay, hiking through the woods, laughing with their friends at the Dairy Top, going to all the sporting events where Cary showed his prowess as an athlete on the field or court. Sarah had always been there to cheer him on from the sidelines. They'd always known what the other was thinking. No one around them ever had a clue about Cary's and Sarah's unspoken conversations.

Sarah heard the clock downstairs chime softly five times before she finally dropped off to sleep. Her dreams were filled with Cary laughing and running towards her and cajoling with all their friends, always in the middle of everything, always the life of the party. No matter the scene, his eyes always found hers and their silent communications would pass back and forth unhindered by those around them.

The dream she awoke from was like a setting from the book, Wuthering Heights; Heathcliff and Cathy running wild on the moors together. But their faces were Cary's and Sarah's. They had seen the movie together and Cary had said it reminded him of the two of them. Yes, it was true they had grown up together making believe all kinds of things as children. As they walked home from the theater, Cary had said, "But our story will be much happier than theirs."

Sarah sat up in bed and wondered if her mind would ever let her rest. Had she really told Millie just a few days ago that she could hardly recall Cary's face unless she was looking at his picture? Now, his animated face was before her as real as life every waking second. This was harder than losing her mother because she and Cary had planned to spend the rest of their lives together.

Something was trying to get into her conscious thoughts, what was that idea at the edge of her mind? She could see herself and Cary standing close together on the porch that last evening when he'd asked her to marry him and he'd given her the ring.

Then Cary had prayed and asked God to keep him safe and bring them back together again. Bam! *That's it, God hadn't kept Cary safe. He had refused to answer Cary's prayer.* Sarah felt something closing up deep inside of her. Like a robot she got up, put her robe on and walked downstairs.

Aunt Fan was waiting for her. She told Sarah that Mr. Evans had called and told her they would be going ahead with a funeral. It would be too hard on Jo Ann to wait and keep hoping that Cary would come back.

"Yes, I suppose so," replied Sarah in a flat tone of voice.

Aunt Fan watched Sarah all morning and became more worried. The light had gone out of her eyes. In a few days she would try to talk with Sarah and help her. She knew it was futile to try just then.

Millie came over later. She had heard the news from Ava. Aunt Fan showed Millie in and told her to go on up to Sarah's room. Fan could hear the murmur of Millie's voice. Occasionally she could hear that Sarah was speaking.

After more than an hour, Millie came down looking very discouraged. "I hope this is just a temporary phase she's going through right now," Millie shared with Aunt Fan. "She seems to have lost her faith."

"When the girls lost their mother," began Aunt Fan, "Sarah became very quiet and withdrawn. She gradually came out of it. It was Cary who helped her the most." The two women looked at each other and wondered if they would be able to help Sarah now.

"We are going to pray, Millie, and we'll not stop praying until our Sarah is back."

Chapter 24

Decisions

MR. HAMLIN WAS at Ava's cabin door again. Ava had decided to keep a low profile. She didn't have to commit to anything, at least not right away. That had always been her mode of operation. She liked to make her own decisions without letting other people persuade her. And she found if she kept her innermost thoughts to herself, she could usually keep the one doing the persuading uncertain of their efforts.

Mrs. Hamlin had taken the bus back home after her visit to Dothan. Ava was not only genuinely glad to see Mom back home, but she also noticed that Mr. Hamlin seemed much more relaxed. He would be less inclined to worry about her and Geoff now that his world was right side up again.

"Good morning, Ava," said Mr. Hamlin. He tried to say it with some warmth in his voice but knew it came out differently.

Julia came running to her Grandpa and brought out his most heartfelt smile instantly. He suggested they go to the patio together and Julia could play in the yard as they visited.

Ava didn't feel inclined to go with her father-in-law and started to say she had to finish the dishes. "Ava," Mr. Hamlin's voice had an edge to it Ava had never heard before. She turned to him. "I have some very important information to give you." He stood there looking directly into her eyes.

Thoughts scrambled through Ava's mind. "Had something happened to Howard?" she wondered. Her heart gave an odd lurch. Anything Mr. Hamlin had to say was undoubtedly unpleasant, but Ava couldn't see any other way but to hear him out.

"Ok, Dad," she agreed. "Julia, you go with Grandpa now and Mommy will be there in a few minutes," Ava directed her daughter.

Happily, Julia took her Grandpa's hand and walked with him, her curls bouncing in the morning sunshine.

Julia was busily playing on the little platform that Grandpa had built to look like a castle. She and Grandma Virginia were having their own animated conversation. Julia had let her princess doll spend the night outside and was carrying her around telling Grandma all about it.

"What I have to tell you isn't about Howard, thankfully. But it will come as quite a shock," warned Mr. Hamlin. "And I don't know any way to ease into it so I will just give you the information. Just before Geoff came here, he had escaped from the POW camp farther north. He is a German soldier." Mr. Hamlin paused to let the words sink in.

He watched Ava digest the news. He could see that she was indeed shocked but beyond that her thoughts were impossible to decipher. He and Virginia had discussed how the news about Geoff would take care of any infatuation Ava felt toward him.

"What's going to happen now?" asked Ava.

Mr. Hamlin knew the authorities would be coming to arrest Geoff soon. He hated to keep that information from Ava but they were at war and Geoff had become the enemy that his son, Howard, was fighting against.

He hoped Ava would forgive him later for not telling her how soon the authorities would be coming to arrest Geoff. He and Virginia had discussed this and they both thought Ava might warn Geoff.

"Ava, please don't tell Geoff that we know who he is. Please trust us to handle this. Will you do that?" He looked at Ava with a mixture of hope and doubt on his face.

"I won't say anything," promised Ava. She owed Howard that much.

Mr. Hamlin got up and called to Julia. "Do you want to walk to the mailbox with Grandpa?"

Julia ran to him. "Let's go, Grandpa." The distance to the mailbox was just the right size walk for Julia's little legs.

Mom Hamlin sat down with Ava and told her about her visit at Nora's and how well she got to know the patrons of Nora's and Jim's grocery store. It had been a special time of bonding with her daughter.

"Mommy, mommy, you got another letter from Daddy," Julia called out as she and Grandpa approached. "And Grandpa and Grandma got one, too."

Ava felt the Hamlins watching her as she took the letter from Julia. Somehow it made her feel guilty. Instead of each of them reading their letters together on the patio as they usually did, Ava took Julia's hand and explained that she needed to have a bath after playing in the dirt. Then they would read Daddy's letter.

Julia forgot about the letter once she was happily playing in the bath. Ava waited for Julia's nap time before reading Howard's letter.

Dearest Ava,

My darling, I miss you more and more. I didn't think my heart could ache more than it has to be with you and Julia. But when I read about our daughter and the cute things she says and saw her picture, it seemed my heart would break in two.

95

I hope and pray she will take to me when I come back. Who would have thought that we'd have a daughter this old who's never met her father?

I'm sorry, Ava, that you've had your young life so twisted up by this crazy war. Please don't forget me.

Sometimes I have a nightmare that you've decided not to wait for me and I see you with someone else. If you wait for me, I promise to make it worth the wait for the rest of your life.

You are the only woman I've ever loved. There's a saying in our family that the Hamlin men are one-woman-men. When we fall for our woman, that's it for life. You are that woman for me, my love.

There are plenty of pretty girls in the places where we sailors have been, but not one of them could turn my head.

I don't think this war will last much longer. Before we know it, we'll be in each other's arms once again.

Kiss Julia for me and show her my picture and tell her I love her, too.

Your loving husband,
Howard

Ava felt the tears falling down her cheeks. How had she gotten herself into such a predicament? She and Geoff had just been two young people being polite to each other. But somewhere along the way she had let her heart go out to him. After that, it became a battle too big for her. She was tired and worn out from the emotional struggle and the sleepless nights. Even though she'd been dutifully avoiding him, she knew deep in her heart that they would have more opportunities to be alone together. And she hadn't forgotten the strong feelings she had felt toward him that day at the beach.

After reading Howard's letter several times, she felt depressed about her fantasies of being with Geoff. Giving in to those fantasies would irrevocably alter her life, and Julia's. She thought about how the news of Cary's death had changed her sister.

Ava never would have dreamed that Sarah could be anything but steadfast and unswervingly obedient to the tasks laid before her. But Sarah had changed. She no longer seemed to care about the importance of relationships in life. It had given Ava a feeling of insecurity to watch her sister flounder. *I need to put Julia first and stay focused on what's important in life.*

Chapter 25

Thoughts and Prayers

GEOFF KNEW SOMETHING had changed between him and Mr. Hamlin. That morning as they worked side by side in the dairy, Geoff had caught Mr. Hamlin eyeing him with nothing less than suspicion.

He'd always known this day would come. He still wanted a relationship with Ava, but she was one woman that kept him guessing. When their eyes met, he could tell she still had feelings for him. He wanted to explain his real identity to her before he took off. Who knows, maybe he could contact her after the war . . . if Howard didn't make it back.

Geoff needed time to think, but time had slipped away like sand in an hourglass. *If Mr. Hamlin found out who I am, then he's told Ava about me.*

Geoff wanted to explain everything to Ava, but would she listen? He hoped she would see that he wasn't a terrible person. Life's circumstances had put him in this predicament.

He had to leave that night. Maybe Mr. Hamlin had reported him to the authorities and they would soon be there. He'd been a prisoner once and he didn't want to be one again.

Since the horseback ride, Ava had been avoiding him. He had thought about it and realized there was nothing else she could do.

As the sun began to set, Geoff knocked at Ava's door and asked if they could talk. Ava's mind was in a whirl. Why did Geoff want to talk with her? Did he suspect that Mr. Hamlin was on to him?

Julia was playing in her room, oblivious to everything but her make-believe session with her dolls. Ava quickly stepped onto the porch and hoped Julia wouldn't notice Geoff's presence. Ava surmised that Geoff was about to take flight and that he'd come to say goodbye. Ava had read Howard's last letter over and over. She had made up her mind that she would wait for Howard and Julia would have her real daddy.

Inside the farmhouse the Hamlins were kneeling at the side of their bed praying. So much was at stake in all their lives. What would happen to Howard if he came home to find that Ava had run off with someone else? In spite of all that Mr. Hamlin had learned about Geoff he still cared about him. They'd spent hours working together. He prayed that things would not go too badly for Geoff when he was arrested.

"I came to say goodbye," Geoff began. She wondered if she should warn him to flee immediately but she had promised Mr. Hamlin that she would trust him to take care of the situation. *Maybe Dad hasn't even called the authorities yet.*

Ava felt confused and was afraid she'd say the wrong thing, so she did what she'd always done in times like that. She would let the other person do all the talking and not divulge her own thoughts. Her silence worked like a charm.

"She must know who I really am," thought Geoff.

"Before I go, I want to explain some things to you, Ava," Geoff began. "I'm not a bad person. The only reason I ended up fighting for the Germans was because I had gone to live with my dad in Germany three years before the war began. My dad wanted me to become a German citizen so that's what I did, not ever dreaming that I'd be asked to fight in a world war in just a few years."

Ava truly was speechless as she listened in fascination to all Geoff was telling her. She wanted to hear Geoff's story so she kept listening as he poured out his heart to her.

"You see," Geoff continued, "I grew up in this country living with my mother after my parents divorced. But when my mom became very ill and couldn't take care of me anymore, she and my father agreed that I would go to Germany to live with him.

"When I turned eighteen in 1941, I was forced to join the army. Thankfully I had only fought in a couple ground skirmishes when I was captured. The Americans brought me to the POW camp here in Alabama.

"I was going to try to talk with the head commander after getting in his good graces. I thought he might listen and help me." Geoff laughed sardonically and continued his story while Ava listened. "I told a buddy of mine at the camp how I'd come to be there and that I hoped to be granted amnesty and be released. He just laughed and said, 'Good luck with that.'"

"I gave up hope and watched for an opportunity to escape. It wasn't that hard. The Americans are far more lenient with their prisoners of war than the Germans. They even provide a library and the men are allowed to play sports. It was easy to get a G.I. uniform. One day when there was a lot of traffic going in and out of the main gate, I just walked out.

"Then I hitchhiked here and found this place and a new life. For some reason, Mr. Hamlin didn't ask me many questions."

"So, what are you going to do now?" asked Ava. "I know Dad cares about you."

Suddenly they both heard cars pulling into the Hamlins' road and Geoff made a split- second decision to run.

"Goodbye, Ava," he quickly kissed her cheek and disappeared into the darkness.

Ava watched military policemen surround Geoff's cabin. They shouted to warn him that they were armed and to open the door. Two officers burst through Geoff's door and Ava heard them shout, "He's gone!"

"Mommy, Mommy," Julia cried. Ava ran to Julia's room.

"Yes, darling, what is it?" Ava said as she reached for her daughter.

"Are the bad men here, Mommy? I heard them."

"No, darling, no. Shh," Ava said as she stroked Julia's hair. She moved to the rocker with Julia in her arms and sang softly to her until she calmed down.

"Being your mom has changed my life," she whispered to her daughter. Julia smiled up at her mom and they cuddled in closer to each other.

Dad and Mom Hamlin had decided to avoid any discussions with Ava that might upset their granddaughter so they stayed in their home after all the excitement. Once Ava and Julia had settled down for the night, Ava said a prayer for Howard and Geoff and all of them. Sleep didn't come for a long time. Knowing she had done the right thing was a new experience she wanted to savor for a while.

Chapter 26

The Island

CARY AWOKE TO the sound of waves lapping on a beach. He felt the warmth of the sun on his back. He looked up from the rough boards he lay on and tried to focus his eyes. The makeshift raft he found himself on had washed up onto the beach but still moved up and down with the waves.

He lay back exhausted and tried to recall the events that had gotten him there. The ship's siren had sounded an alarm just before the explosion. Cary could remember absolutely nothing from that moment on. How he'd managed to survive and wash ashore on a few scraps of wood he had no idea.

"I'm alive," he thought, "but where am I?"

He heard a movement nearby and turned his head to see a dark-skinned woman watching him. They continued staring at each other. The young lady looked half afraid of him and stood back from the raft.

Cary spoke to her, "Please don't be afraid. I won't hurt you. I need help." He tried to get up but fell back down. His head hurt so badly that it made his vision blur.

The woman ran to his side and knelt down. She spoke a foreign language. He motioned to her that he couldn't understand.

She stood up and took hold of his arm to help him up. She motioned with her hand inviting him to come with her.

He allowed her to help him up and the two moved slowly across the beach. Cary's head pounded with every step he took.

The woman's arm was around his waist and he leaned on her as they entered a small clearing with a few huts. Palm trees waved in the breeze. Cary heard some voices calling and the lady at his side answered back. "This must be paradise, but it doesn't feel like it," was Cary's last conscious thought. Then everything went black.

Two days later, Cary awoke in a small, thatched hut. He heard voices outside speaking what sounded like Spanish. He tried to get up but the effort made his head hurt so much that he lay back down. Soon a young lady came in. She looked vaguely familiar, but Cary couldn't remember where he'd seen her.

Chapter 27

The Cat Family

IT HAD BEEN a week since Geoff's flight. Ava had been listening to the news on the radio. She had asked Sarah to keep an open ear for her as well. It seemed too awkward to discuss Geoff's situation with Mr. and Mrs. Hamlin. Sarah wondered why Ava was so keenly interested in the disappearance of the Hamlin's hired man, but she agreed to let Ava know if she heard any news of Geoff.

Ava wanted to talk with Dad and Mom Hamlin but she hadn't been able to bring herself to apologize to them. The four of them had tried to put the past behind them and continue as though it had never happened. But that wasn't working very well and the awkwardness they all felt was making things tense.

Julia in her own perceptive way would say, "We're a happy family, aren't we?" when the elephant in the room loomed too large. Ava knew she held the key to restoring peace and she determined to get things cleared up for Julia's sake. Otherwise she and Julia would have to go live somewhere else.

One evening when Julia was happily playing in the yard, Ava asked her parents-in-law to join her for a glass of lemonade. Mom Hamlin took her apron off and said that sounded like just what she needed. She and Mr. Hamlin followed Ava out to their patio.

They sat down and sipped their lemonades and tried to think of a few innocuous things to say about the day. They'd hired a teenage boy to help with the cows for the summer.

Finally, Ava cleared her throat and began, "Dad and Mom, I need to apologize to you for putting you both through so much when Geoff was here. I realize now how obvious it was that we were flirting with each other and I had no business doing that. I feel embarrassed and ashamed." Ava could hardly believe she was saying these things. Having Julia to put ahead of her own needs was causing a metamorphosis in her life.

Virginia cut into Ava's thoughts, "Oh, Ava, we know how hard it is for you to talk about what happened and we really do appreciate this apology. And I think I can speak for both of us and say that we forgive you."

Mr. Hamlin wholeheartedly agreed.

"I also want to say," continued Ava, "that I really do love your son. I miss Howard very much. I can't wait for him to meet Julia."

"Mommy, Grandpa, Grandma!" called Julia excitedly. "Look, look!" Julia was pointing at the kittens that Mama Kitty was leading across the yard.

"Well, would you look at that," said Mr. Hamlin. "Mama Kitty has finally decided to let us meet her kittens. I knew she'd had them but she wasn't telling where she had them hidden."

They all got down at Mama Kitty's level so they could meet her kittens. Grandma rewarded Mama Kitty by bringing out a bowl of milk for her.

"What should we name them?" She asked.

"Let's see," said Grandpa, "this one needs a boy's name and so do these two. Only this little one will have a girl's name. She's the only tortoise shell, just like Mama Kitty."

Julia squealed with delight over the soft little kittens. Ava told her to handle them ever so gently.

After some deliberation, they decided the gold kitten would be called Tiger. The black one would be Coffee. The other two had Mama's tortoise shell pattern. The male would be called Tip for the gold tip on his tale and the female they named Essie. Mama would be known from then on as Mama Kitkat.

Julia said, "We're a happy family, aren't we?" and they all laughed. Julia wouldn't need to say it anymore because now it was true.

Chapter 28

Millie's Friendship

MILLIE AND SARAH decided to do another day trip, this time to Gulf Shores. Millie hoped that getting out of town for the day would help Sarah to begin to enjoy life a little again. Sarah had tried to give Cary's car back to his parents, but they had only said they knew that Cary would want her to have it. So, once again they set out in the Ford Coupe.

The drive was very scenic along the back roads of Alabama toward the Gulf of Mexico. "There's just something about getting out of town that makes one feel so free, don't you think so, Sarah?" asked Millie. "I feel all my cares roll away."

"Yes, I know what you mean, Millie," replied Sarah.

Millie had to be somewhat careful what she said around Sarah now. She wanted to talk about how the Japanese were being pummeled in the South Pacific and that the war could be over by Christmas, but she thought better of it. Letters from John were still arriving at the Ledoux home and Millie was beginning to have real hope that he would come back in one piece.

Millie's heart ached for Sarah as she watched her friend struggle to regain some sense of normalcy. She had quit coming to church and that was something Millie had never thought would happen.

Working at the high school seemed to be the best tonic for Sarah right now. Sarah had even offered to work extra days as things got a little busier toward the end of summer in preparation for the upcoming school year.

Aunt Fan had patiently waited for Sarah to talk with her about her grief but that hadn't happened. She and Millie continued to pray for Sarah.

"Have you seen Ava lately?" asked Millie. Sarah had confided in Millie about all the drama in Ava's life. Ava had finally told Sarah about her short emotional entanglement with Geoff. Millie could be trusted not to pass the information on to anyone else.

"Does anyone know what happened to Geoff?" Millie asked.

"He seems to have disappeared into thin air," replied Sarah. "Ava came by a few days ago, with Julia of course. We all had lunch together and walked to the park so Julia could play. Ava is different now. She truly does seem to have grown up."

"I've noticed that, too," answered Millie. "I've seen her and Julia at church. I think Ava works in the nursery."

Sarah didn't know what to say. It seemed like a role reversal for her to be avoiding church and Ava to be getting more involved. Nothing was the same since she'd received the news of Cary missing in action.

At Gulf Shores, the girls found a place to park at the beach. They got their swimsuits and beach blanket out of the back along with the picnic basket Mrs. Ledoux had packed and walked toward the changing rooms.

A lot of young ladies were wearing two-piece swimsuits, but Sarah and Millie felt too funny showing their midriff in public. They came out of the dressing rooms and looked for an empty spot on the already crowded beach. People loved to cool off at the Gulf in the hotter months of summer. The breeze coming across the Gulf made the hot muggy days a little more bearable.

"It still seems strange, doesn't it, Millie, that it's mostly women on the beach?" Sarah observed. "Most of the guys out here are still in high school," she added.

"I know, we couldn't have imagined it if we'd tried," was Millie's reply.

"But the women sure are showing off their figures. I can't believe how skimpy the suits are getting," Sarah said.

"Like your Aunt Fan says, 'What's the world coming to?'" quoted Millie.

Sarah and Millie were getting looks from some of the young men as they laid out their beach blanket. Even in a modest suit, good figures were still easy to spot.

"One thing I do seem to have going for me," said Millie, "is a nice figure. Of course, those young guys over there are probably just looking at you, Miss America." Millie laughed at her joke.

Sarah barely glanced at the guys that were grinning in their direction. *Who cares?"* She smiled benignly at Millie's compliment.

They ate the goodies Millie and her mom had packed. "Now we have to wait for at least thirty minutes," informed Millie.

Sarah laughed. She'd been hearing that rule all of her life. "One must wait thirty minutes before swimming after eating a meal." Millie giggled at Sarah's mimicry.

A boy about fourteen came by and asked if they would like to rent an umbrella for fifty cents. "Will you put it up for us?" asked Millie.

He readily agreed to do that, so they paid the fifty cents and had a nice shady refuge from the broiling sun.

Sarah had spent plenty of time at the ocean since moving to Fair Pointe to live with Aunt Fan. It felt good to frolic in the waves. It made her feel happy and sad at the same time. She had always loved being knocked down by the powerful waves. But the waves couldn't erase the ache in her heart. Instead they brought back memories of Cary's laughter.

Still Sarah had to admit that it seemed right to be revisiting one of her favorite places. And she was glad to be with Millie again. Neither one of them wanted to think about the brutal war that continued to wreak havoc across the Atlantic Ocean.

The water was so warm that they stayed in longer than usual. Finally, when they felt too tired to stand, they collapsed on their beach blanket and looked up at the blue sky. Sarah and Millie lay there listening to the sound of the waves crashing and the call of the seagulls. Neither of them felt the need to talk.

Millie looked over at Sarah and saw that she'd fallen asleep. *There's nothing like the beach to calm a person's nerves,* Millie philosophized to herself. She smiled knowing her friend was getting some good therapy.

On the way home, Sarah began to open up with Millie. She hadn't done that since she'd gotten the news about Cary. Sarah wasn't used to feeling at odds with her creator. She never had before. It hadn't been a pleasant experience the past few months. She hadn't been speaking to God and her strength had always come from her relationship with Him.

Sarah's immature faith had been stunted when Eliza died three days after the car accident more than nine years ago. But Sarah had been a girl then. And Cary had come along just when she most needed his friendship.

Millie sensed that Sarah wanted to talk. She and Aunt Fan had been praying for this crack in the armor Sarah had put up around her heart. *Go slowly, Millie,* she warned herself.

Sarah began to share some things tentatively. It reminded Millie of a rabbit coming out of its warren. As soon as it perceives danger, it scurries back to its den. Millie didn't want Sarah to "scurry back inside herself."

Millie heard a little voice in her head telling her to be a good listener. That meant no philosophizing and no lecturing.

"The first two weeks after we got the news about Cary, I felt numb," explained Sarah. "But every night I dreamed that Cary was with me and that we were on one of our exciting explorations through the woods or in his motorboat on the bay. Then I'd wake up and remember that he's gone. All I could do was put my feet over the side of my bed and force myself to get up." Sarah glanced over at Millie and then back to the road.

"Seeing Aunt Fan's look of concern made me feel like an extra twenty pounds had been put on my back to carry around all day. Not that I blame her, but for the first time since we came to live with her, I couldn't meet her expectations as I'd always done. I've been feeling like I shouldn't live with her anymore because it's too sad for Aunt Fan to see me this way. I know it's hard for you too, Millie. I'm sorry."

"Sarah Suydam, don't you ever apologize to me for being your friend. I love being your friend!" Then Millie remembered to let Sarah talk.

"I know, Millie, and I love being your friend, too," Sarah conceded. She felt a little warming around her heart after speaking good words to someone she cared for, something she hadn't been able to do for a long time.

"But my thoughts lead me to the same dead end every time," continued Sarah. "I always end up on our porch with Cary's hands resting on my shoulders and I hear him say it all over again, 'Lord, please keep me safe and bring us back together.' Why wouldn't God answer his prayer, Millie? Why did God have to take him? Why do I lose everyone I love, first my dad, then my mom, and now Cary?"

For once Millie didn't have a philosophical answer. She silently prayed for God to help her know what to say. After a few minutes, Millie spoke quietly, "I don't know the answers, dear friend, but I do know that God loves us and He makes all things work together for good . . ." Millie's voice got even quieter as she finished, ". . . to those that love Him."

They drove along through the great Southern forest with the sun casting its shafts of light like spears through the great trees.

"Maybe that's it," Sarah reasoned, "maybe I've never really loved Him." Millie knew better than to argue with Sarah's doubt.

111

Chapter 29

Good News

HOWARD THOUGHT HE must be dreaming. The doctor at the hospital on Saipan had just informed him that he was being sent home. Howard had never felt such a searing pain after he dove into the foxhole to take cover from incoming enemy fire.

"I think I've been hit, Juan," Howard yelled in his buddy's direction. His fellow combatant lay Howard down in the dirt and looked for blood. He didn't see blood but what he did see made him want to vomit. Howard's left arm seemed to have grown two inches longer than his other arm. Howard's eyes had a glossy sheen as his body went into shock from the pain.

When the enemy fire ceased, Juan yelled, "Medic!!" They'd gotten Howard to the field hospital where the x-rays showed the humerus bone completely severed. The surgeon on duty informed Howard that Someone must have been watching over him because the break was a clean one without splintering of the bone. Howard's entire arm was put in a cast to restrict movement and allow the humerus bone to grow back together.

The doctor gave him something for the pain and Howard was taken to a cot to rest while he waited for the paperwork to be completed for his journey homeward. The pain wasn't diminished nearly enough but Howard could have shouted for joy – HE WAS GOING HOME!

The commanding officer told his assistant to make the call to Howard's family that he would be sent home due to a broken arm. If only Howard could talk with Ava. He longed to hear her voice as he lay there in pain.

Ava heard both Dad and Mom Hamlin calling to her. She opened her door and saw them running across the yard toward her cabin. She'd never seen either of them run before and the sight almost made her burst out laughing. Julia was sitting in her highchair working on a sandwich. But she knew something was up and her bright eyes were taking it all in.

"Ava, we have the most wonderful news," cried Mom. "Howard is coming home!"

"What? Is the war over?" Ava felt joy flooding her heart and wondered if it was too good to be true.

"No," replied Mr. Hamlin as he continued taking deep breaths. "Howard's arm was badly broken and the doctors decided to send him home."

Ava turned around to Julia and yelled, "Honey, your daddy is coming home!!" She ran over and lifted Julia's tray over her head and picked her up. Ava danced around the cabin with Julia in her arms. Dad and Mom Hamlin were beaming and clapping for joy as they watched their girls celebrate.

When Ava stopped whirling, Julia looked at her Grandpa and Grandma who had tears of joy streaming down their faces. "Why are Grandpa and Grandma crying Mommy?" asked Julia.

More laughter filled the cabin and Ava hugged her daughter, "Those are tears of joy, honey. Sometimes when people feel this happy all they can do is cry," she explained. Julia looked puzzled. She would have to think more about that one.

For the next week, Ava and Howard's folks talked often to Julia about her dad to help prepare her to meet him. Julia wanted her daddy's picture next to her bed. Every time Ava saw it she wondered if Howard would still look like the carefree young man in the picture.

A week later, Virginia hurried to get Ava. "Howard's on the phone, Ava. Come quick."

Ava and Julia ran across the yard to the house as fast as Julia's legs would go. Mr. Hamlin handed the phone to Ava when she came through the door.

"Howard?" cried Ava. "Where are you?"

"Oh, darling, it's heavenly to hear your voice," said Howard. "I'm in New Orleans and will be getting on a bus tomorrow to travel the rest of the way. The schedule has me getting to Fair Pointe at 6:00 p.m."

"Oh, Howard I can hardly believe it!" Ava was grinning at her in-laws as they hung expectantly on every word.

Howard gave her as much news as he could in the few minutes they had to talk. He wanted Julia to hear his voice.

"Julia, come here honey," Ava called. "Daddy wants to talk to you." Grandpa picked her up and brought her to the phone.

Ava held the receiver to Julia's ear. "Julia, this is your daddy, sweetheart. I'm on my way to you. I'll be there tomorrow. Will you be there to meet me?" Julia looked at her mom and Ava nodded her head yes.

"Yes, Daddy," Julia solemnly vowed.

Ava and the grandparents laughed at her big eyes as she spoke to Howard for the first time.

As soon as Ava got off the phone the three of them began to plan for Howard's welcome the next day. "Let's call our family and friends," said Ava "and have everyone come out to meet him."

"I'm not sure that's such a good idea, honey," warned Mr. Hamlin. "Howard may not be ready for that many people yet."

"Oh, I hadn't thought about that," replied Ava. "Maybe you are right."

In the end they decided to just invite Sarah and Aunt Fan to join them at the bus depot the next day. There would be plenty of time for a welcome home party later.

Chapter 30

Howard's Family

HOWARD HAD BEEN dozing off and on while the Greyhound bus traversed the countryside headed east. His body was gradually learning to relax. As the intensity of pain in his arm lessened, it seemed all he wanted to do was sleep.

But as the bus got closer to Fair Pointe, the excitement gave him a rush of adrenaline. Howard took out his most recent photo of Julia and gazed down at it.

"She's beautiful," the older lady next to him said. "Is that your little girl?" she asked.

"Yes," Howard proudly showed her Julia's picture. "They're waiting for me in Fair Pointe," he told her. "It will be the first time I've seen her."

"That's so wonderful," the lady said. "It's nice to hear a few happy stories these days. Although it looks like you've not been having a very good time."

The rest of the trip passed rapidly as Howard and his seat mate chatted amicably.

At home, excitement was mounting as Howard's loved ones prepared to welcome him home.

Julia felt the festive mood and her curls were bouncing more than ever as she hopped and ran and giggled. Finally, Ava and Grandma grabbed their handbags and whisked Julia through the door. Grandpa was sitting in the car like a ticking bomb waiting for the women to come out and get in.

The same pandemonium was taking place at Aunt Fan's house as she and Sarah made several trips to the car practically bumping into each other. They had prepared food for the family celebration at the Hamlins' farm.

"That's everything," Sarah said on her last trip to the car. She handed the dish to Aunt Fan in the front seat. "Here's the German potato salad." They both looked at each other and started laughing. "Well, the German kind is the best, after all."

Aunt Fan and Sarah pulled into the depot's small parking lot a few minutes after the Hamlins. When Julia noticed her Granny walking toward them, she ran toward her. Aunt Fan bent down and picked Julia up.

"Granny, my daddy is coming!" Julia cried.

"Isn't it wonderful?" Aunt Fan kissed the little girl's soft cheek. They quickly joined the others.

"Here it is!" shouted Mr. Hamlin. With her usual foresight, Aunt Fan handed Julia back to Mr. Hamlin.

The bus's brakes squealed as it came to a stop. It seemed that the doors would never swing open as they stood there waiting, the smell of combusted gasoline filling the air. Julia watched excitedly from Grandpa's arms, looking at the bus and back at her mom's face and then back to the bus.

The driver had asked everyone to please allow the servicemen to exit the bus first, not that he needed to tell them. As Howard and two others walked to the front of the bus, everyone stood. The civilian men removed their hats as the sailors made their way forward. As anxious as Howard was to have his wife and daughter in his arms, he was deeply touched by the show of gratitude. He would never forget it.

The doors opened and Howard stepped down and into Ava's arms. He lifted her in his good arm and swung her away from the door where he planted a long, firm kiss on her lips.

Everyone on and off the bus broke into cheers watching the sailors greet their loved ones. Julia immediately joined her voice with the others. Howard looked at his daughter's glowing face and felt love well up inside of him. He didn't want to ever let go of Ava. Julia was leaning away from Grandpa toward her parents with her arms outstretched. Howard and Ava looked at each other and laughed as they both realized that he could only hold one of them at a time. He let go of Ava and Julia came into his arms. In that moment, the long nightmare came to an end.

Julia looked into her daddy's eyes and seemed to understand the importance of the moment. She watched the tears rolling down her daddy's cheeks. "Mommy, is Daddy crying for joy?" Julia asked innocently. Julia wondered why everyone was suddenly laughing. And why everyone seemed to have tears of joy.

Sarah had no thoughts for her own happiness as she basked in her sister's joy. And she knew that Ava had almost missed this. One more false step and her sister might not have been here to greet her husband.

"Daddy needs to hug Grandpa and Grandma and Granny and Aunt Sarah," Ava told Julia. Howard drew his mom close and held her. Then Howard turned toward his dad. He couldn't remember ever seeing his dad cry before. Aunt Fan and Sarah hugged Howard gingerly, afraid to hurt his arm.

They were all talking at once as they made their way across the parking lot to the cars. Mr. Hamlin carried Howard's bag and Howard held Julia.

"See you at the house," Ava called to Fan and Sarah.

Chapter 31

Normal and Abnormal

LIFE SEEMED A little more normal now that one of their men had returned home from the war. Sarah and Aunt Fan visited often with the Hamlins. They were planning a welcome home party for Howard to be given one week after his arrival.

Howard had fared better than he might have, his parents noticed. They remembered how troubled many of the returning soldiers were after World War I and wondered how their son would adjust to civilian life. Would he have nightmares and wake up screaming in the night? Would he suffer from hallucinations that brought back war scenes?

They began to breathe easier concerning their son after he'd been home for a week and seemed to be fine. Julia had quickly become Daddy's girl and it was as though the two of them had never been apart. Ava smiled whenever she saw them together and silently thanked God that she hadn't made a terrible mistake.

Howard helped as much as he could around the farm. He could still sit a horse and help Salt and Pepper round up the cows for milking. Mr. Hamlin had expanded the operation just before the war when he purchased more dairy cows and had better milking machines installed.

Ava called to Howard from the yard, "I'm going to go to Sarah's for a visit. Could you come in while Julia finishes her nap?"

Howard thought he could use a nap himself and was only too happy to oblige.

Ava parked Howard's Buick in front of Aunt Fan's and went up the walk. Sarah was talking on the phone when Ava came in and waved to her sister.

Aunt Fan was listening to the latest news on the war. Ava could hear the newscaster's voice saying, "Because of the danger of the German flying bombs, over 41,000 mothers and children left London in the second wartime exodus from the city and returned to their former wartime billets in the country."

Ava hated to be reminded that the war was still going on now that Howard was home.

Next, she heard the announcer say, "Adolf Hitler departed Berchtesgaden and flew to the Wolf's Lair."

Aunt Fan could see that Ava was irritated so she turned the radio off. "What, no Julia this time?" she asked.

"Not this time, Auntie," replied Ava. "She and Daddy will happily keep each other company."

Sarah got off the phone and came into the living room.

"Who was that, Sis?" Ava asked.

Sarah looked at Ava and wondered how much to tell her. "That was Thomas. Remember he was at your wedding, Ava."

"Oh, was he that handsome blond man that stood and talked with you and Cary for a while?" *Rats, there I go mentioning Cary again.*

"Yes, that's right."

Ava and Aunt Fan were both looking at Sarah expectantly. "I know you two won't leave me alone until I tell you why Thomas called me. So, yes, Thomas asked me out and I told him I would go."

"That's good, Sis. It's about time you had some fun again," Ava encouraged.

Aunt Fan decided to withhold judgment until she could see this Thomas herself.

"Speaking of having fun, Sarah, why don't you come to church with Aunt Fan this Sunday and see Julia in the patriotic program the kids are doing? I've seen a couple of their practices and it's so adorable."

"I'll think about it," Sarah replied in a tone of voice Ava had never heard before.

Ava was staring at Sarah. "Why are you looking at me like that?" Sarah asked.

"I miss you, Sarah," she looked sad. "I used to be so jealous of you, Sis, because you always wanted to do the right thing. In fact, it drove me crazy. But this new person you've become . . . it's like you aren't even Sarah anymore. Please come back soon, Sarah."

Sarah turned on her heels and went upstairs. Ava and Aunt Fan tried to visit for a while longer but soon gave up.

Chapter 32

Island Life

CARY SAT NEAR the fireplace where all the hot meals were cooked. He had cleaned the grouper that he and Maria's cousin, Cayo, had caught that morning. The fish was sizzling over the fire while Maria and her mom finished slicing the mangos. The pita bread had been fried in coconut oil and smelled delicious.

Maria smiled at Cary. Their ability to communicate had improved quickly once Cary was able to be up and about and hear people talking. Maria's family and the neighboring relatives had immediately tried to bridge the communication gap. Cary recognized many of the words from his Spanish high school class. He surmised that Maria's people spoke some dialect of that language. *That makes perfect sense because this island must be part of the Canary Islands that are part of Spain. Thanks, God, for bringing me to shore in a neutral country.* He'd heard about the barbaric conditions American POWs faced in German camps.

Maria's mom, Ana, looked over at Cary and then back to Maria, "Lo esta hacienda mucho mejor ahora." (He's doing much better now.)

"Si mama, no es maravilloso? Cuando vino por primera vez no saviamos si viviria." (Yes Mama, isn't it wonderful? When he first came we didn't know if he would live.)

Maria's dad, Jose, sat off to the side whittling until dinner was ready. Jose was a quiet man. Cary was never sure what Jose thought of him. Normally he could read a man pretty well but Jose kept his thoughts to himself. What Cary did know was that Jose always seemed to be watching him.

Cary had tried to tell Maria that he needed to get to a town and let his loved ones know he was alive. But so far he hadn't been able to make her understand the urgency of getting news to his family. Cary didn't even know if there were any phones on the island. Maybe it wasn't an island at all, but surely his miracle raft must have washed up on one of the small islands in the Canary Islands.

He had to get to a town once he got stronger. His concussion was nearly healed but he still didn't have the strength to walk very far. He would just have to wait.

After months had gone by Jose, Ana and Maria still didn't seem to wonder what they should do about their visitor who'd shown up so mysteriously. Cary could see that the three of them were very happy that he was better. As Cary watched these people go about their daily lives of finding and preparing food, he realized they didn't worry about anything else. *Why would their new friend be any different?*

After they finished the simple meal, Cary told Jose that he was going to visit los primos. Maria's young cousin, Cayo, had become like a little brother. Cayo was teaching Cary how to whittle a piece of wood into a work of art.

Cayo had also clued Cary in about one of their strange customs. Cayo liked to call it, "catching a husband." Fifteen year old Cayo had noticed how Maria liked to follow Cary around. He wanted to do a favor for the man he looked up to so he told Cary to beware of finding himself alone with Maria.

If they were found in a compromising position which meant being alone together, and Cary didn't want to marry her, Maria could take the matter to the elders. After the elders heard both sides of the story and heard one or two witnesses, they could make the man marry the woman who had been compromised.

The old Cary would have laughed over such a preposterous situation as he found himself in. What was it his psychology teacher used to say? "It's easy to think lightly about the misfortune of someone else until it happens to you." Cary had never felt more helpless in his life.

The cove these islanders lived in was accessible only by water. He thought about Sarah and how she must think he had perished in the explosion. Somehow he had to get word to her. *For now all I can do is pray.* Pastor Redding with his dry sense of humor would say, "Oh how awful, has it come down to that?" *Yes, Pastor, it has.* Cary smiled at the memory.

"God, if there's some way you can let Sarah know I'm alive, please do." He felt like a little kid asking God for such a miracle but with all the props removed, Cary found that God was his only hope.

Chapter 33

Aunt Fan Remembers

THOMAS PULLED UP in front of Aunt Fan's. *What a quaint little place* he thought as he hopped out and headed for the door. Aunt Fan opened the door and he immediately felt that he was being scrutinized from head to toe.

"Hello Miss Ferguson," Thomas gave his best smile which usually brought a smile to the recipient's face. Thomas's smile faded slightly as he regarded Aunt Fan. *Hmm, this one might put a fly in the ointment.*

"Come in," said Fan in a clipped voice. Thomas stepped inside and perched on the sofa while Aunt Fan called up to Sarah that her date had arrived.

Thomas's heart skipped a beat when he saw Sarah. She had an evening gown on and looked like one of the Miss Americas he'd seen in a contest in New Jersey. "Wow," he almost said before he noticed Aunt Fan regarding him very intently. Instead, he said, "Hello Sarah, you certainly look lovely this evening."

"Hello Thomas, shall we go?" Sarah let Aunt Fan know about when she'd be back, not because she had to; her aunt would worry otherwise.

After Thomas had Sarah safely tucked into his sports car, he forgot himself and squealed the tires as he pulled away from the curb. "Thomas, slow down," cried Sarah, laughing. She suddenly felt young and carefree again. The thrill of danger had always intrigued her.

Aunt Fan sat down on the porch and shook her head. *I never thought I'd have to wonder about Sarah. What is she getting herself into?*

People thought of Aunt Fan as a stolid, middle-aged woman who'd never had any experience with men. They were so wrong! Fan saw herself at Sarah's age when Floyd would pick her up and whisk her away. He'd pull up in his Ford T Bucket sports car and Fan's dad would look completely annoyed at all the noise that car made.

Floyd had caught the attention of most of the young ladies at Fair Pointe High School and Fan was so proud that he had asked her to go out. Fan's parents didn't feel comfortable with Floyd but they had always let their only child, Fan, do what she wanted to do. So, they watched uneasily to see where the relationship would go.

If only my parents had sat me down and told me how they really felt, maybe they would have saved me a lot of heartache.

Fan recalled how Floyd always made her feel like a queen when she was on his arm. Everywhere they went, others would crowd around them. The girls envied her position as Floyd's girl and the guys envied Floyd for having the guts to ask Fan out. She'd always seemed aloof and stuck up. Floyd had seen what the others had missed – that Fan was trying to cover her insecurity by playing hard to get.

Their senior year in high school, Floyd and Fan were inseparable. They were the couple in the spotlight at the sporting events and parties and proms. Fan had a background in ballet that made her a dream on the dance floor. Floyd had gotten the prize he'd set his eyes on.

Floyd had learned that he could get on better in life if he kept his innermost thoughts to himself. *So like Ava.* Inside he was a wounded little boy who'd been abandoned by his dad at age eleven. He'd never gotten close to the couple that posed as his parents. They were too straight-laced for Floyd. He and his dad had lived a very carefree life on the road after his mother had passed away when he was seven.

Floyd had learned a lot about impressing people just by watching his dad. Then Jacob had left Floyd with the Millers one day and Floyd never heard from him again.

When Floyd was in high school, even in junior high, he began to realize that he had a knack with people, just like his dad. He could easily get on someone's good side and they'd be falling over themselves to give him what he wanted. It seemed ridiculously easy to Floyd, like taking candy from a baby.

There was something Floyd liked a lot about Fan. She wasn't just another pretty face. She had a depth to her. He thought she was a prize worth pursuing. The lost little boy inside of him was drawn to Fan's wholeness. Floyd had found a way to break through Fan's reserve and win her heart.

Toward the end of their senior year, Fan expected that Floyd would ask her to marry him after graduation and they would spend the rest of their lives happily ever after. But something big happened that spring that changed her dreams.

Her parents asked Fan to sit down one afternoon. They had something to tell her. She knew by their unusual behavior that it was something big.

Her mother explained to Fan that, due to unforeseen circumstances, Uncle and Aunt Ferguson needed a temporary place for their daughter, Eliza, to stay for a while. Fan wondered what in the world such circumstances could be, but personal matters were not discussed openly in their family. Her parents would tell her if they wanted to. They explained to Fan that Eliza would be coming to live with them. They asked Fan if that would be all right, but Fan knew it had already been decided.

Fan felt excited. She'd have the sister she'd always wanted! Fan and her mom prepared a bedroom for Eliza while Mr. Ferguson made a trip to escort his niece back to Fair Pointe. He drove north to Montgomery and took the train to Chicago. Eliza would be traveling by train from Ellensburg, Washington, to Chicago.

Fan remembered seeing Eliza once when they were little girls. She was very pretty with big blue eyes and silky blond hair. In fact, when relatives had come for Eliza's funeral and seen Sarah for the first time, one of them commented, "Why, there's Eliza right there."

After Mr. Ferguson returned with Eliza, Fan took an instant liking to her. She truly felt that she had the sister she'd always wanted. Soon Eliza was going everywhere with Fan and Floyd. It didn't matter that Eliza was two years younger. They loved having her along on their outings. Fan appreciated Floyd's being willing to have Eliza tag along and the Fergusons could relax knowing that Fan had a chaperone. What could go wrong?

Fan knew where the memories were taking her, but time had healed her wounds. It had been ages since she'd thought about any of it. Something about Thomas had jogged her memories of Floyd.

Floyd and Fan brought Eliza to the last dance of the school year. Some of the senior guys had brought a stash of liquor. They'd go out to their cars and have a few drinks and then come back in to dance. Harold, one of the seniors, had his eyes on Eliza and became more and more attentive to her. He wanted Eliza to dance every dance with him. Some of the guys were getting fed up with Harold monopolizing her.

Floyd finally decided to come to Eliza's rescue. Aunt Fan could almost laugh over it from her vantage point twenty three-years later. Harold had drunk too much, and he didn't take kindly to Floyd telling him to leave Eliza alone.

Soon the two of them were tumbling across the dance floor. The girls screamed and the guys hooted and hollered for Floyd to clean Harold's clock. Floyd had only managed to sneak out for one drink so he soon had Harold flat on his back.

Nothing was the same after that. Fan soon realized that Floyd looked at Eliza differently and Eliza was completely smitten with her hero. As time went by Fan knew she couldn't hold onto Floyd any longer. Their outings were an excuse for Floyd and Eliza to be together even though they were still playing their parts as though nothing had changed.

At first Floyd denied his interest in Eliza but Fan wasn't going to let him keep up the charade. When Fan confronted Eliza, Eliza told her that she wouldn't date Floyd even if he asked her. Fan knew that resolve wouldn't last once she was out of the picture. She realized that Eliza had never intended to fall for Floyd or to capture his heart.

After graduation, Fan had to get away from Fair Pointe. Her heart was broken, and her pride was sorely wounded. The gang she and Floyd had run around with talked behind their backs. She looked through the want ads and saw a position to be a nanny to two young children in Jacksonville. Fan told her parents that's what she wanted to do and called to arrange going to apply in person for the position. Fan's parents had observed all the changes, but true to their pattern of glossing over touchy subjects, they never tried to discuss it with her. In a way, Fan was glad. Perhaps it made it a little easier.

Fan took the Greyhound to Jacksonville, was hired, and began her job as nanny immediately. For the next two years she buried herself in the lives of the two children. The parents were very wealthy and the home she lived in was like a mansion. There was unlimited money for Fan to entertain the children any way she saw fit.

The Fergusons drove to Jacksonville occasionally to visit her. Fan heard news of the happenings in Fair Pointe from time to time. She told herself she didn't want to know about Floyd and Eliza, but morbid curiosity got the better of her.

During the Christmas season, a friend relayed the news to Fan that Floyd and Eliza had eloped. Fan suspected that Eliza would be having a child before nine months rolled around, and she was right. Sarah Grace Suydam was born July 10, 1922. The couple had settled in Longview, Texas, where Floyd was hired on by the railroad.

A little over three years later Ava was born. When Ava was still a newborn, Floyd abandoned Eliza and the girls. Eliza called Fan when she realized that Floyd would not be coming back. She needed moral support.

The two women became close again, this time through correspondence. Fan had moved back to her home in Fair Pointe and was able to take the bus to Longview once or twice a year to visit Eliza and the girls. From Fan's first visit, Sarah and Ava knew her as Aunt Fan.

After Floyd left, Eliza had taken a secretarial position at the Land Bank and managed to support her girls . . . until the day of the accident.

Aunt Fan looked around her be-flowered porch and wondered how long she'd been reliving the past. *How near I came to having the same fate as Eliza. How ironic I was spared from the very thing I thought I most wanted.*

Chapter 34

The Party

THOMAS CAME TO an abrupt stop in the circular driveway of an elegant mansion in Fair Pointe's wealthy neighborhood. Sarah tried not to look awestruck as she took in the opulence all around her. The large yard was immaculately groomed and the house looked at least five times larger than Aunt Fan's. Ornate statues and sculptured shrubs decorated the large portico at the front of the three-story home. Marble pillars marked the entrance. Sarah could see people in glittering clothes moving about through the floor-to-ceiling windows. She was glad that Thomas had told her to wear a nice evening gown. This place surpassed the elegance of the Lawrences' in Tallahassee.

"Thomas, do you show up at the homes of the rich and famous at every town between Mobile and Tallahassee?" Sarah teased. She would have to be on her toes tonight and stay on them. She did wonder how Thomas, whose father owned a trucking company, had come to move in such elite circles.

As if Thomas had read her thoughts he said, "Uh, by the way, Sarah, please don't mention that I'm a truck driver. In fact, my step-father has decided it's time for me to start advancing in the company. From now on, I'll be learning what all goes on in the office. Before long I should be running the company."

"Oh, don't worry, your secret is safe with little-old-me,"

Sarah said demurely. She would have to tell Millie about her night life adventure with the wealthy. She almost giggled at the thought. Thomas was looking at her as if he wasn't too sure he wanted to introduce Sarah to these socialites.

Thoughts were racing through Sarah's mind as Thomas watched her. *What's gotten into you? You are acting the way Cary used to. He always did like to poke fun at people's pride, and what made it even funnier was those pompous souls hardly ever knew they were being made fun of. Maybe I miss him so much that I'm beginning to act like him to keep his memory alive.*

As soon as they entered the large foyer, Thomas felt pride welling up inside him to have Sarah on his arm. The men's heads began to turn as soon as they saw her. For a minute Thomas thought a hush had descended over the crowd.

"Thomas, my man," said a distinguished person who appeared to be about twenty years older, "Who is this beautiful woman on your arm?"

He turned to Sarah and did a little bow from his waist. "I don't believe I've had the pleasure of making your acquaintance my dear." Sarah was annoyed with herself as she felt her face get hot. She could just imagine how red it must be turning.

"This is a friend of mine," laughed Thomas, "and her name is Sarah. Sarah, this is Jacque Du Bois. Sarah remembered hearing the name. Mr. Du Bois was one of the wealthiest men in Alabama.

Thomas realized just then that there was nothing more by way of introduction to say about his beautiful date. He couldn't say, "She's a secretary at the local high school." But Thomas felt certain that if Sarah was smart and didn't say too much, her beauty would assure her success. He liked the new Sarah much better than the one he'd first met. The new Sarah was more sophisticated and socially adept.

"Oh, there you are, dear," drawled a gorgeous woman with a huge diamond on her finger. "Jacque, please introduce me to your new friends."

Sarah found it difficult to look elsewhere than at the woman's generously endowed figure. Sarah averted her eyes and noticed that Thomas didn't have any such qualms. In fact, she'd never seen him display his glistening white teeth so unabashedly. Jacque introduced his wife, Guenevere, to Thomas and Sarah. Sarah noticed how Guenevere looked at Thomas and smiled as though she knew something about him.

Thomas deftly kept them moving through the crowd. He seemed to know quite a few of the couples and introduced Sarah as they made their way across the room toward the dance floor.

Sarah realized the less she said the better chance she'd have of coming across the way Thomas wanted her to. *Was this Thomas's way of testing her - bringing her to a mansion filled with high-society people?*

Thomas was a true socialite. He could converse with anyone and make them think they were talking to somebody worth talking to. Sarah admired that about him. It wasn't her forte and she liked to watch the Thomases of the world in action. Cary had been the same way.

The band music was playing the popular new swing songs and the dance floor filled with couples who had taken the time to learn the steps. Sarah whispered to Thomas that she didn't know how to dance to the swing music. He guided her to a small table where they could watch. A waiter came by and Thomas took two drinks off the tray for them. Sarah looked at the goblet of sparkling punch and hoped it wasn't spiked. Thomas laughed into her eyes, knowing what she was thinking.

When the song, "I'll Never Smile Again," began playing, Thomas took Sarah's hand and pulled her to her feet. "Come on, Sarah, you can dance to this song. It's slower. I'll guide you."

As they moved gracefully around the dance floor, Sarah noticed a few females looking at them and whispering. "Thomas, those women over there are talking about us," Sarah pointed out.

Thomas looked in the direction Sarah intimated, and she thought she saw a fleeting look of panic swiftly pass over his features. "Oh, let them talk," Thomas whispered in her ear. "They're probably saying that we're the couple to watch."

Sarah did feel like a princess as Thomas swirled her around the dance floor. After she'd watched the couples doing the swing style for a while, Sarah told Thomas she thought she could do it. Thomas took her outside to a patio even larger than the one in front so they could try out the new steps. Lanterns hung from tree branches and Sarah thought she'd never seen anything so beautiful.

A few couples were standing at the edge of the veranda talking quietly, some were stealing kisses. After Thomas showed her the basic swing steps, he said, "Sarah, you're a natural born dancer. Let's go back inside and show 'em what we've got."

Sarah laughed as she let Thomas pull her back into the ball room. They danced the rest of the night and Sarah wondered why she hadn't done a lot more dancing. She and Cary had always gone on outings with their friends that were mostly outdoor activities like hiking or swimming or boating.

During the band's intermission, Thomas and Sarah filled a couple plates with food and found a table. The man at the next table was telling an interesting story. People had stopped to listen. Thomas and Sarah found themselves listening as well.

"I tell you it's the truth," the man said. "His family all thought he'd been killed. There were very few survivors after the ship was torpedoed and sunk. A year later, the guy shows up alive. It turned out he made it to a remote island where the islanders nursed him back to health. But when he got back stateside, his fiancée had married someone else."

"George, you're telling tall tales again," hooted one of the men. Everyone laughed.

"You can laugh all you want," the man answered. "But it's true none the less."

Thomas looked at Sarah. She had turned white and seemed to be miles away. "Where are you, Sarah?" Thomas whispered. He knew she had to be thinking about Cary. It was inconceivable to him that he could lose her now just when they were having such fun together. He'd never failed to conquer any woman's heart before. Suddenly Thomas knew he wanted Sarah more than anything else and he'd do anything to have her.

Chapter 35

Millie's Advice

SARAH HAD A restless night. The dreams of Cary returned. A bright light woke her at the crack of dawn. It was only a shaft of sunlight shining through the edge of the curtains. But it was as good as an alarm clock.

Sarah lay on her bed trying to remember what she had dreamed. She knew the dreams were about Cary but there was nothing her mind could grab hold of.

She thought about the evening she'd spent with Thomas and the feeling of magic as they glided across the dance floor. People had watched them and admired them. For a few hours, Sarah had felt like a modern Cinderella.

But the clock had gonged the midnight hour noisily in her ear when they'd heard the man telling the story about the sailor found on an island. Sarah wondered if God had sent her a message. Was Cary alive?

"I have to talk to someone," she thought.

"Good morning, Aunt Fan. I want to give Millie a call and then I'll join you for a cup of coffee."

Aunt Fan turned the radio off and watched Sarah make a light breakfast of toast and fruit. "There was an attempt to assassinate Hitler," she informed Sarah. "Unfortunately, it failed."

"How can such a madman have escaped this long?" asked Sarah.

Aunt Fan wanted to tell Sarah about the liberation of the first concentration camp, Majdanek, but knew Sarah was still consumed with her own issues. The deplorable conditions of the survivors were too horrible to talk about.

"Millie says to come over in about thirty minutes," she informed Fan.

The two of them went out to the porch to enjoy its ambience before the day became too hot. Fan was half afraid to ask Sarah about her evening with Thomas. She so wanted Sarah to talk with her the way she always had but that seemed to be a thing of the past.

"How was the party last night?" Fan finally asked.

"You should see that mansion, Aunt Fan. I've never seen such opulence, both inside and outside. I thought the Lawrence place was amazing but this was like something out of the movies.

"Most of the people there dripped of wealth. Either this war has padded their pockets or the great depression didn't affect them that much." Sarah didn't really want to tell her aunt about the dancing. That was something Aunt Fan had never encouraged.

"We had a good time, but right now I better get ready and get to Millie's," Sarah quickly got up and took her dishes inside.

Fan would just have to keep waiting and praying for a breakthrough. Surely Sarah would come to her senses again. "Oh Lord, please don't let her heart be broken," she prayed softly.

Mrs. Ledoux had gone to the grocery store, so the girls sat in the living room at Millie's. "Oh this is luxury," said Millie. "Sometimes I want to tell you something so badly at work, but there are too many listening ears."

I know," agreed Sarah. "I need your advice, Millie. You know Thomas took me to the Du Bois' party last night." Sarah could tell Millie wanted to hear all about it. Sarah had to fill her in on the people she saw, what they said and what they were wearing. And she told her how much she'd enjoyed the dancing.

"Oh, John and I had a lot of fun dancing at a barn dance one time," said Millie. "But that was square dancing." Sarah almost laughed but realized in time what a special memory that was for her friend.

"Have you heard from him lately, Millie?" Sarah genuinely wanted to know. Her own news could wait a few minutes.

Millie went and got John's letter and read parts of it to Sarah. "He makes it sound as though he knows he'll be coming home before too long, doesn't he?" asked Millie.

Sarah thought about the news of Hitler managing to escape the assassination attempt and decided not to tell Millie about it.

"Okay, enough of that," said Millie. What's your big news?"

Sarah carefully explained the man's story of the rescued sailor. Millie's big brown eyes looked bigger than usual when Sarah finished. "What are the odds, Millie, that Thomas and I would have sat right there where I could hear that story? Do you think it was meant for me to let me know that Cary is still alive?"

"Oh wow," Millie looked unsure of what to say. "It was a very unusual thing to have happened," she said. "My gut reaction is to believe that it's a sign from God, but at the same time I hate to get your hopes up."

"But why would God go out of his way to let me know if Cary is alive, because I, well, you know I'm not close to God anymore," Sarah finished lamely.

"This reminds me of the Sunday school lesson I taught the kids. One of the teaching points was that when they do wrong and their parents aren't happy with them, does that mean they don't belong to their parents anymore? It's the same in our relationship with God. Once we've opened our hearts to His Son, we are His child and nothing can ever change that."

Sarah believed what Millie said but she wasn't ready to pursue that line of thinking yet. "Yes, you're right, Millie. But what should I do? If I stop seeing Thomas, he may never come back and what if Cary is dead? I will always love Cary but Thomas is a lot of fun. I forget life's problems when we're together."

Millie knew Sarah wasn't ready to pray about it, but she could pray for her. Then she thought of some good advice she could offer her. "If I were in your shoes, Sarah, I would tell Thomas that you and he can only be friends. Tell him you owe it to Cary to wait until the war is over before you commit yourself to someone else."

Sarah quietly thought about Millie's idea for a few minutes. "You know, I think you're right, Millie. That might be the only solution there is for now." Sarah felt like a load had fallen off her shoulders.

Chapter 36

Jean is Angry

OVER THE NEXT few weeks, Thomas continued to visit Fair Pointe to be with Sarah. If he didn't have enough gas rationed to make the drive from Tallahassee, he could use the excuse of taking a shipment to Mobile and stop in Fair Pointe on the way back.

Thomas decided to play along with Sarah's idea of their just being friends. If that's how it had to be, he would bide his time. Since Sarah insisted that she and Thomas always meet with friends, word got around quickly that they were an item. Sarah knew it was futile to argue with people.

As she wondered what to do on a Saturday morning, she knew she could no longer put off going to see Cary's parents. It seemed like their getting together would just make things sadder for all of them. But she was determined to do it for Cary because that's what he would want.

Sarah drove the Ford Coupe to the Evans'. She had called ahead to let them know she was coming. Pulling into their lane and driving through the middle of the pecan orchard brought back so many memories. In her mind's eye she saw Cary, Jean and herself playing tag in the orchard. As adolescents, the three of them preferred outdoor adventures. Looking for alligators in the back-wood swamps seemed more interesting than going to the matinee downtown with their peers.

Hide and seek was a favorite of hers and Cary's when the neighbor kids showed up. They had their secret hideouts where no one could find them. They would spy on the others and laugh as they watched them search.

None of the others, including Jean, could climb trees and scramble over barn roofs as well as she and Cary. When they lay flat on the barn roof and someone started climbing up to check it out, they would scamper to the lower shed and leap to the soft dirt below. Sarah imagined she could hear the voices and laughter of childhood as she drove up the lane to Cary's house.

Sarah got out of Cary's car and slowly walked to the back door. Mrs. Evans opened the door and hugged her. The two of them felt tears filling their eyes but Sarah hadn't come to cry. She had a desperate need for life to be as normal as possible and hoped the Evans would understand that.

The three of them visited for a while. They told Sarah who would be helping them with the pecan harvest and Sarah found innocuous things to tell them about different folks they both knew. Lots of things happened around the high school - always a safe topic. Mr. Tuxbury, the history teacher, had finally asked Miss Trummel to marry him. They planned to marry in the spring and hoped the war would be over by then.

Jo Ann chuckled as she remembered, "Cary always said that Mr. Tuxbury had a terrible crush on the Spanish teacher, but he didn't know how he'd ever get his courage up enough to let Miss Trummel know it."

They heard a car pulling up on the gravel outside and Mr. Evans pulled the lace curtains back to see who it was. "It's Jean, Mother. She was able to make it after all."

Jean came in through the back door and joined them in the living room. Sarah noticed that Jean seemed cold and distant.

The conversation that had been going pretty well suddenly felt awkward and tense.

"Has something happened at work that you need to discuss, dear?" asked Jo Ann.

"Oh, no, Mom, just the usual dramas. All the Rosie Riveters are still vying for the affections of the foreman. Although, I don't think I told you that he fell and broke his leg so now he has to get around in the factory on crutches. It did hamper his style but the ladies feel sorry for him so that worked in his favor."

Silence once again filled the room. Sarah felt oppressed by Jean's presence. She recalled Jean's old habit of sulking when something bothered her. Eventually she would explode and release her wrath on the one who had offended. Sarah needed an excuse to leave.

"Howard and Ava are joining us for lunch. I haven't seen Julia for a while. She's changing so fast. Sorry I can't stay and visit longer." Sarah smiled warmly at Mr. and Mrs. Evans as she drew near to hug them goodbye.

She approached Jean to hug her, but Jean said, "Oh, I'll walk out with you, Sarah. I'll be right back, Dad and Mom," she called over her shoulder.

Jean cut right to the chase once the two of them were outside, "Sarah, what's all this I hear about you and Thomas seeing each other? You only got the news about Cary six months ago and you're already dating? I can't believe it," Jean glared at her.

Sarah hadn't even been sure why she agreed to see Thomas that soon herself. She didn't know what to say to Jean. She had felt so lost after finding out Cary was gone. And Thomas showed up and wouldn't take no for an answer.

"You know how people exaggerate, Jean. Thomas is only a friend. In fact, I told him that I don't want to get involved and that we could only be friends," Sarah explained. It made her angry that she had to explain her life to Jean.

Jean's glare softened to an uncertain look. "You know, Thomas has a reputation of being a lady's man," Jean informed. "One of the bosses I work with at the shipyard saw you and Thomas dancing at the Du Bois mansion a few weeks ago. He thought he recognized you as Cary's fiancée, so he told me about it. Would you like to know what he shared with me about Thomas's previous affairs?"

Jean didn't wait for Sarah to answer. "He's been involved in several scandals, including an affair with a married woman. Supposedly another woman took him to court for child support and claimed that Thomas is the father of her child. Thomas isn't paying child support and says that he's not the father. Is this the man you are choosing to replace Cary?" asked Jean.

Sarah felt as though she'd been slapped. She couldn't defend Thomas because she knew nothing about any of those rumors. And, sadly, Sarah realized she couldn't defend herself either. She hadn't been making very good choices since she'd launched out on the sea of life without her heavenly Guide.

But as she stood facing Cary's sister, Sarah didn't feel inclined to agree with her. Jean had the accusatory look on her face that Sarah had always hated. Sarah knew Jean was probably right but instead of agreeing with her she found herself saying, "Do you make it your business to go around overseeing everyone's lives, Jean?"

Then Sarah turned away and quickly got into her car. As she accelerated down the gravel driveway, she saw a cloud of dust envelope her accuser. It felt like justice to Sarah.

Chapter 37

Desperation

CARY WALKED ALONG the beach. The sun had disappeared over the cliffs toward the west and darkness gradually spread over the waters. It was time to make an attempt to get off the island. But he'd only met with dead ends in his mental calculations. He had learned that the island was called El Hierro. He needed a map to know where the towns were located. *I can't ask for a map. They'll know right away what I'm up to.*

Cary had managed to avoid being alone with Maria in spite of all her efforts to corner him. He knew that Ana would like nothing better than for Cary to marry her daughter. They had nursed him back to health and taken care of him, sharing their food and home with him. Cary didn't want to hurt them. He had hoped that somehow his leaving could end well but he knew that wasn't possible.

I haven't done anything to encourage Maria but I never encouraged the girls in Fair Pointe either and that didn't deter them. He and Sarah would mimic the latest girl hot on his heels and laugh their heads off. That was before they'd reached the point of no return when their childhood friendship had suddenly morphed into something bigger than they could have known.

Cary's mastery of the Spanish dialect had increased rapidly as he heard and spoke it every day. *Miss Trummel would be proud.*

I wonder if Mr. Tuxbury ever got up his courage to ask her for a date?
Cary had to smile a little.

Thankfully, language was no longer the obstacle. Jose and
Ana would do whatever Maria asked them to do. Cary had to get
her to persuade Jose to help him. "Please make her understand,
Lord," he prayed as he walked back to his hut. Cary wondered
what Sarah was doing that very moment. *Has she started seeing
anyone?*

The next morning, Maria met Cary and her father at the
beach as they brought their catch in. They'd gone out in Jose's
sailboat early to get the fish they'd need. After they pulled the
boat onto the sand, Jose walked away with the string of fish for
Ana to clean and prepare.

The beach was one of the safe places for Cary to talk with
Maria. There were always people coming and going. "Podemos
hablar?" He led her over to a fallen tree where they could sit
down. "Maria," Cary continued in Spanish, "I must get off this
island. I have to get home. Will you help me?" His black as night
eyes pleaded with Maria.

Maria looked very unhappy. "Why do you want to leave us,
Caurree, aren't you happy here with us?"

"Maria, you saved my life and for that I will be forever grateful.
You will always have my friendship. But I've told you that there's a
young lady waiting for me at home that I have promised to marry.
I will do anything I have to do to get back to her."

Cary had decided to work every angle to try to make Maria
understand. She was young, still a teenager. He hoped she would
come to see it as an act of noble love to let him go. Someday
she'd marry one of the islanders and be able to forget her childish
crush on him.

Maria got up and stomped away from him. Cary put his head
in his hands and groaned, "Lord what now? Who will help me?"

Chapter 38

The Charmer

SARAH FELT ANTSY as she waited on her porch for Thomas to pick her up. She knew that she was playing with fire. She had told Thomas they could only be friends, but she sensed her resolve slipping away. Dancing in his arms every weekend had given her feelings that were out of her control. Fan stepped out to the porch.

"You seem jumpy tonight, Sarah." Sarah noticed that Aunt Fan had changed her tactics. Instead of looking worried when she looked at Sarah, she simply looked calm. Somehow her aunt's calmness made Sarah feel even worse. Aunt Fan's letting go simply made Sarah realize that it was her own life she was toying with.

After Jean gave Sarah the inside scoop about Thomas's past, Sarah was surprised to find she felt a certain intrigue. She knew things about Thomas that gave her an advantage, or so she thought. It became like a good game of chess. Thomas continued his charade of being the good guy who'd come to give Sarah everything she wanted. But was it just a charade or did Thomas care enough about her to become a new man? Sarah had to admit that she'd been enjoying living a little dangerously. *With Cary gone, what do I have to lose?*

When Sarah saw Thomas's sports car pull up out front, her heart began pounding. This was a sure indication that she was losing her resolve. If Thomas were just a friend, her heart wouldn't be beating like this. But as with all the other warning signs she'd received, Sarah wasn't ready to stop playing the game.

If Cary were alive, she would stop seeing Thomas immediately. But she had no way of knowing for certain that the story she'd heard at the Du Bois mansion was a message from God or not. She couldn't forget what she'd heard that night. The man's words haunted her. *If you are alive, Cary, you better come back soon before all the sand slips through the hourglass.*

Looking more confident than she felt, she blew Fan a kiss and headed toward the fancy car where Thomas waited for her.

"All things that aren't right must come to an end," she heard Fan say, "and sooner is better than later." Sarah let the words evaporate into the sky.

"She's in your hands, Lord," and Aunt Fan went inside to have some dinner alone in the quiet of her kitchen.

Lately Thomas had been taking Sarah to a dance every weekend. He always knew where the best bands were playing. Sarah especially liked it if they had to drive out of town in Thomas's sports car with the top down. She liked watching the sunlight fade and Thomas would tell her funny stories about learning how to run a trucking company. On their way back to Fair Pointe the stars would be shining brightly in the night sky. She would miss the out-of-town trip tonight since their social set was meeting at the Fair Pointe Dance Club.

Thomas drove through downtown Fair Pointe and turned the corner around the Dairy Top. As they drove past Sarah saw Millie sitting with Doris and Margaret at one of the patio tables. Millie glanced up along with everyone else who heard the fancy car passing by. For a second hers and Millie's eyes met. Millie started to wave. Then her hand seemed to stop in mid-air as if she'd waved at a ghost.

Sarah felt badly that she hadn't been spending much time with Millie. She needed to do something about that. The last time she and Millie had gotten together, Sarah had felt ashamed of herself. Millie was waiting for John to return and had been completely faithful. She wasn't running off to dances, instead she had continued to attend the auxiliary club to make things for the soldiers. Sarah had gotten so busy with Thomas that she'd stopped attending the meetings. *Men are fighting and dying and here I am running around to parties and dances every weekend.*

"Why so glum, chum?" laughed Thomas. He turned the radio up a little louder and the swing music grabbed hold of Sarah. She seemed to enjoy dancing more than anything these days. Her feet started keeping time to the beat and she couldn't wait to get on the dance floor.

Soon they pulled into a parking space a block from the door of the dance club and Thomas came around and opened Sarah's door for her. She held his arm as they walked to the club. Sarah still wasn't used to wearing high heels.

Soon Sarah was laughing and enjoying herself, dancing to some of her favorite songs by Artie Shaw and Benny Goodman. Thomas had been good about not having more than one glass of wine on their dates but Sarah noticed that he was imbibing more than usual.

"Hey Tommy," called Sam, "let me dance with that beautiful doll. Don't be greedy."

Sarah felt Sam pull her gently away from Thomas. He was as good a dancer as Thomas and Sarah relaxed as they did the swing steps in perfect unison. When the song ended, Sarah looked around for Thomas and saw him at a table with two women she didn't know.

Sarah walked toward the table and saw Thomas lean toward the gorgeous brunette by his side and whisper in her ear. Sarah felt hot anger swelling up inside of her.

"Fine," she thought, "if that's what he wants to do I'll leave him to it."

Sarah grabbed her jacket and walked up the stairs into the night air. The music followed her. As Sarah stood on the dark street and listened to the raucous laughter emanating from the club, she suddenly felt like Cinderella had lost her ball gown and was shivering in her tattered servant rags. She remembered one of Aunt Fan's sayings, "Not all that glitters is gold."

Taxis were pulling up getting ready to take some of the partyers who'd had a few too many drinks back to their homes. Sarah walked over to the nearest cab and asked the driver if he would take her to 302 Washington Street.

"Sure thing, Miss," and Sarah got in.

As the cab pulled away from the curb, Thomas came running toward it yelling, "What do you think you're doing, Sarah?" She turned away and told the driver to keep going.

The next morning Thomas called to apologize. He was his sweet self again. He asked Sarah if they could go to dinner that evening. She declined. She needed to take a breather and rethink some things.

Thomas managed to bite his tongue before the angry comment he wanted to throw at her could escape.

Chapter 39

Ava's Questions

SARAH SAT BY herself on the sunny porch. She had always loved late February because spring was about to bring back all the vibrant colors of the south. The holidays had been dreary for her, something she just had to get through; except for the times when Julia's happiness had been contagious. A general malaise seemed to have settled over Fair Pointe as everyone tried to cling to the hope that the war would end soon. The women Sarah knew who still received letters from their boyfriends and fiancés seemed nervous and edgy as though their "good luck" might not hold out long enough.

Sarah had continued to go out with Thomas, but not as frequently. The night at the dance club had been a wake-up call. He tried to persuade her to go dancing again but Sarah had decided to take a break from dancing. She'd found out that two people who dance together are destined to become lovers. Her plan to just be friends hadn't worked.

Thomas hated to admit defeat, but he was getting tired of trying to resurrect the old feelings in Sarah. In fact, he'd started dating a couple other women but hadn't told Sarah yet. He was back to playing the field with women. Thomas had returned to the dance clubs in Tallahassee and Mobile while he waited to see if Sarah would come around to his way of seeing things.

Sarah mused over what to do about her life as she waited for Aunt Fan and Ava's family to return from church. It had been months since Sarah had gone. Aunt Fan had relayed Pastor Redding's phone message for Sarah when she'd first stopped attending. He had wanted Sarah to call him and set up a time when they could meet. He wanted her to know he was there for her. But she had not returned his call.

Sarah could hear Julia's happy voice before she saw them turn the corner walking toward Aunt Fan's. She was delighted that her parents had let her walk home with Granny and had kept Fan laughing most of the way with her refreshing observations.

Sarah could hardly believe all the changes in her sister since she'd gotten married and become a mother. She was truly happy for Ava that she had settled down. How ironic, thought Sarah; I've given Aunt Fan more to worry about the past year than Ava.

Howard and Ava pulled up in front and Julia began running toward them from the other direction. Howard stood on the sidewalk waiting for her. Julia giggled as Howard swung her up high and turned in circles. Ava stood there smiling as she watched them. Seeing Howard swing Julia around brought back a similar memory to Sarah. Once upon a time she had been the little girl in her father's arms. She let out a sigh and got up to meet them.

Aunt Fan went inside and got the roast beef out of the oven. Sarah had mashed the potatoes and set the table. Soon they were all seated in Fan's dining room and conversing easily. Sarah appreciated that they didn't try to make her feel guilty for not going to church. She had to admit that being with her family who loved her unconditionally felt better these days than trying to keep up with Thomas's life in the fast lane.

After dinner, Ava put her sleepy little girl down for a nap. Howard had dozed off on the couch and Aunt Fan had retired to her bedroom to rest.

"Can you believe it, Sis?" asked Ava. "Looks like we get to have a one-on-one visit just like old times."

They brought their iced teas outside and relaxed in their favorite chairs. It reminded Sarah of being with Millie. She would call Millie and see if they could get together soon.

"I love being Howard's wife and being a mom," said Ava. "But sometimes I do think it would be nice to have a little more freedom like you."

"Trust me, Sis, you don't want to change places with me," Sarah replied. It could have been a cynical comment, but Ava noticed Sarah's voice didn't have that bitter edge to it that she'd been hearing since the news of Cary had ripped Sarah's life apart.

"You know I was thinking about you the other day," continued Ava. "I was wondering why you'd been able to keep your relationship with Cary on a friendship level all those years while I, on the other hand, didn't do so well. I know Howard and I are right for each other, but I wish we'd had a better start and done things right. Anyhow, I really am curious, Sis." Ava hoped Sarah was in the mood to divulge some of her secrets. Ava had doubted if she should bring up Cary's name, but she knew her sister was quite taken with Thomas.

"Well," began Sarah, "you know that Cary and I were just kids when we started hanging out. And mother had died which gave me a very sober outlook on life at a young age. I got used to Cary just being there. He was my best friend. Then when we got into high school and all the cool girls started chasing him, it seemed comical to me."

"Okay, I get that," said Ava. "But I know somewhere along the way you started having real feelings for him. Cary always wanted only you. Yet you always played hard to get."

"To tell you the truth, Ava, I didn't want to end up like our mom. You were younger and didn't realize many things she went through. I can remember hearing her cry in the night when she thought we were both asleep. Her life was so hard and I'm sure she either missed Floyd very much or regretted ever falling for him. Who knows, maybe she'd fallen for some man at work and knew it could never be."

"Wow!" cried Ava. "I never thought about Mom wanting to be with another man. All she did that I remember was work and take us kids hiking or swimming sometimes on the weekends."

"Well, all I'm saying is that there are things we just don't know about our mother."

"Yes, I suppose you're right." Ava looked thoughtful. "Now that I'm a mom I appreciate what she sacrificed for us a lot more.

"Okay, so that's the story with Cary but what about keeping Thomas at arm's length? He has a reputation for being pretty persuasive with the women."

"Ava, if you weren't my sister, I'd be telling you to mind your own business," Sarah scolded. "If you must know, Millie gave me some advice about waiting and not getting too involved with Thomas." Sarah told Ava what had happened at the dance club. "That verified what Jean had told me about Thomas's previous affairs. You'll be happy to know that I no longer go dancing with Thomas and I don't see much of him anymore."

"Most of the women I've heard about don't usually get out of the spider's web once they've been caught," Ava pointed out. Ava's words sent a little shiver down Sarah's spine.

Just then they heard a little knock at the patio door from inside. Julia was peeking through a crack. "Hi, Mommy," she said.

Sarah and Ava both laughed and assured Julia that she was welcome to join them. Sarah smiled to herself. *What a little character she is.*

Chapter 40

The Stranger

"VICHY INTERIOR MINISTER Pierre Pucheu received a guilty verdict and a death sentence today for his collaboration with the Nazis." The phone rang and Aunt Fan got up and turned the radio off.

"Hello," Fan said into the phone.

"Is this Fan?" At the sound of the voice, Fan felt a sudden jolt. After so many years, she still remembered his voice.

"Yes," she managed to say, "This is Fan."

"Fan, this is Floyd." He waited, not knowing what she would do. Perhaps she would simply hang the phone up or give him a piece of her mind. Either way he deserved it.

Fan couldn't think of anything to say. In shock, she heard herself say, "What do you want, Floyd?"

"I want to meet with you and talk about the possibility of my seeing Sarah and Ava." There was something calm in Floyd's voice. Fan thought he sounded like a different man than the one they'd known years ago. Maybe even Floyd had been changed by the events of life.

Fan thought about Sarah. *She wants to reconnect with her dad.* Sarah hadn't mentioned her dad since they'd gotten the news of Cary's ship being torpedoed.

"I don't think it's a good idea for you to come over here, Floyd. But I will meet you somewhere," answered Fan.

"Thank you, Fan. I know I don't deserve your giving me the time of day, but I want you to know how much I appreciate this. I know it's very sudden. Would it be possible for you to meet me this afternoon at the city park?" *Just like Floyd, always spur of the moment.*

Fan had an instant flashback to the times when she and Floyd would sit in the park and watch the world go by, laughing and talking. But of course, it was the only logical place to meet where the neighbors' curiosity wouldn't be aroused.

"What time?" asked Fan.

"Will right after lunch be all right?" asked Floyd.

"Yes, I'll be there," and Fan hung up the phone. *He didn't say where to meet.* She would go to the bench where they'd always sat. *Maybe he remembers.*

A few hours later, Fan approached the bench in the park and saw Floyd sitting there. He stood and took off his hat with a slight bow. *He still has good manners.*

"Hello Floyd," she said as she held out her hand. He took her hand in both of his and they sat down.

Fan noticed that Floyd had aged very little. He was still a good-looking man even though his hair was receding and he had a few lines on his face. She felt very glad that the years hadn't changed her too much either. She still had her trim figure and very few wrinkles. Her hair was only beginning to turn white. Floyd wiped a stray tear and looked away.

"First of all, Fan, I want to apologize for the way I treated you." Fan bristled thinking that she'd escaped him, and poor Eliza had borne the brunt of his poor choices. But Floyd was still talking, "I ruined Eliza's life and I can never make that up to her."

I guess he does know Eliza is gone. That must be why he called me. They talked for a long time. Two hours later, Fan walked home slowly, mulling over everything Floyd had told her about his life for the past two decades. Sarah was already home when Fan walked through the back door.

"Where have you been, Auntie?" asked Sarah. "It's so strange to come home and not find you here. You look tired, are you all right?"

"I met with someone today, Sarah, and I will tell you about it. But first let me see if Ava can join us." Sarah listened as Fan called Ava and asked her to come over. Sarah felt that something momentous was about to change her life again.

The suspense as they waited for Ava made Sarah nervous as the two of them made a simple dinner and sat together at the kitchen table. Instead of eating, Sarah was drumming her fingers on the table. Fan knew it was futile to tell Sarah she should eat and to please stop drumming on the table.

Chapter 41

Preparing Themselves

AUNT FAN HAD told Ava that she should plan to be away from home all evening. Howard was glad to take care of Julia. Everyone was in suspense and wondered what in the world could have practical Aunt Fan acting so mysterious.

After Ava arrived, Fan suggested they sit in the living room. Ava and Sarah sat down and waited for Fan to let them know what this meeting was about. Fan looked very nervous and uncomfortable before blurting out, "Girls, something big has happened. Your father has returned."

She could not have shocked Sarah and Ava more if she'd said, "I've decided to sell my house and move to Timbuktu." But the Fan they knew didn't make up stories.

The girls continued staring at Fan as though she'd just sprouted horns. Finally, Ava said in her old flippant tone, "Aunt Fan, I think you just said our father has returned. I don't see him. Where is he?"

Hearing Ava's sarcasm gave Fan the indignation she needed to get her going. "Yes, that's what I said, dear girl." Fan then launched into the events of the afternoon. Sarah and Ava listened in amazement. Floyd, their long-lost father had called Aunt Fan? Then she'd gone to meet him at the park?

Fan finally stopped and said, "Say something, girls. You both look like you don't believe a word I'm saying. I assure you it's true. I haven't lost my mind!" The frustration in Aunt Fan's voice loosed Ava's tongue again.

"Auntie, we're sorry for being so slow to respond, but you're right, this is huge news." Ava looked at Sarah trying to read her thoughts. "Sarah, what are you thinking?"

Sarah didn't believe in miracles but here was the biggest one of her life staring her right in the face. "I want to believe it, Aunt Fan. I always hoped this day would come. But now that it's happening, it's hard to realize. Besides, where is he? What if he changes his mind and disappears again before we get to see him?"

"Girls, when I met with Floyd at the park, he wasn't the same man your mom and I knew years ago. He's changed. He has faith now. He wants to see you and be part of your lives more than anything."

She shared more of what Floyd had told her that afternoon before saying, "Ladies, I've told you all I can. He wants to tell you the rest himself."

Floyd and Fan had decided that it would be better for the girls to meet him as soon after receiving the news as possible. "No one will get any sleep tonight anyhow so we (Fan blushed a little at the use of the pronoun 'we') thought it would be best if Floyd comes here to meet you this evening."

Sarah and Ava looked at each other and back at Aunt Fan. What could they say?

Sarah tried to calm her heart as they waited to meet their dad. Questions raced through her mind. What would her dad look like? Would she remember him? What would he think of her? On and on it went. She and Ava paced about Aunt Fan's like caged tigers.

"Why don't you two go upstairs and brush your hair?" suggested Fan. "You need something to do. Floyd should be here in about fifteen minutes."

They squeezed into the small bathroom together and watched each other in the mirror as they combed their hair. "Should we put lipstick on?" asked Ava. "What if he's like Auntie and doesn't think women should wear make-up?"

"Maybe it's better if we don't," Sarah replied, "at least for this first meeting." They did want to look their best to meet their father. They had often fantasized about what it would be like to see him and now it was about to happen.

Sarah recalled how the gardener at the Lawrence's had stared at her through the window. Then Millie saw the picture of Floyd and said he looked just like the gardener. *How could my dad see me and not talk to me?* Sarah felt anger, excitement and frustration all at once.

"Ava, if that man doesn't get here soon, I think I'm going to come apart at the seams," cried Sarah.

"I know, I know," was all Ava could say. They had decided to wait upstairs in the bedroom they had shared.

"Let's pray," suggested Sarah. When she looked up at Ava's face, her sister looked like she was about to cry.

"Yes, let's," replied Ava. "It's so good to hear you say that, Sis."

Sarah smiled at her sister and lead out in prayer as she'd done so many times through the years. "Lord, help us as we meet Floyd, I mean, our father. Help us know how to act and what to say and what not to say. Just help us, Lord, and I'm sorry I haven't talked to you for a long time," Sarah prayed.

"Aunt Fan says he's very repentant for what he did to us, so let's try to remember that," Ava suggested.

"Right," agreed Sarah.

A knock sounded on the door downstairs and the sisters stood perfectly still listening for the first sound of their father's voice.

Chapter 42

Disclosures

ONCE FLOYD WAS inside and they heard Fan's voice asking him to sit down, the girls came down the stairs. Floyd looked at them and was overcome with emotion. He'd had every intention of keeping his emotions under control. But when he saw Sarah and Ava, he couldn't stop the tears.

Aunt Fan stepped toward the three of them as they faced each other. "Floyd, these are your daughters, Sarah and Ava. Ladies, meet your father."

They smiled but no one moved. They were all uncertain of what to do next.

"Please, girls, come sit down and let me talk with you," Floyd stepped back and they stepped around him to the sofa. "Then you can decide whether or not you want to hug me," Floyd said with very little hope in his voice.

Aunt Fan started to go into her bedroom, but Floyd stopped her. "Fan, please, you have been a mother to these girls, and I want you to be here with us."

"The very first thing I must say to you, Sarah and Ava, is how very sorry I am that I haven't been part of your lives. I hope in time you both will be able to forgive me. If I could do it all over again, I never would have left your wonderful mother and you girls.

"Your mother always wanted me to read the Bible and pray with her. She was a dear Christian lady. I was young and foolish and didn't want anything to do with religion."

Floyd continued his story while his daughters listened. They were finally finding out what had become of their father. Floyd spared them many of the details of his sordid life. "I was always searching for something, never able to stay in one place.

"After hearing about the accident and Eliza's death, I started drinking more heavily and ended up living on skid row in Seattle. Everywhere I went I was always asking about my dad, your grandfather, Jacob. When I first left Longview, I traveled to Los Angeles with the idea of finding him. After long months of asking and searching, I gave up. To this day I don't know what happened to him.

"By then I was so ashamed of myself for having abandoned you girls, that I didn't think you'd ever want to see me. I kept believing the lies in my head and didn't know where to find truth. I'd found out that Fan had brought you girls here and I knew she would be the very best person to care for you. But that's no excuse. I'm so, so sorry." Floyd put his face in his hands and quietly cried.

The girls wanted to comfort him, but they felt paralyzed. Finally, Sarah said quietly, "I always hoped you'd come back someday."

Floyd looked up through his tears and smiled. He tried to regain his composure and continue. "Sarah, you were the cutest little doll and I adored you. I've never been able to drink enough to forget your sweet little face when you'd look at me with so much trust and love."

These were the first words that touched Sarah's heart and she felt the tears forming in her eyes. "I have happy memories of you, too," she said. "I couldn't remember your face, but I remembered how you would lift me up high over your head and swing me around."

Ava sat listening and began to feel left out. She'd never been able to know her father at all because he'd left them when she was a baby. *How does a man leave his little baby girl?*

As if Floyd had read her thoughts, he turned to Ava and reached out his hand for hers. "I was such a heel to leave you. Even as a tiny baby I could see that you looked so much like me. Maybe I was afraid that you would be like me in more than just looks." Ava was able to smile at him and remembered her words of advice to Sarah about forgiving.

Floyd didn't want to tell Sarah that he'd seen her and not talked to her, so he left that out of his story. But seeing her that evening in Tallahassee had shaken him badly. She reminded him so much of Eliza. That was the beginning of his undoing.

"One day I knew I'd hit rock bottom and that I couldn't go on and I remembered your mother's plea that I turn to the Lord. So, I walked into a Gospel Mission and asked for help.

"They took me in and I began to attend the Bible meetings. Before long I realized that I was indeed a sinner who needed to repent. I should have repented a long time ago but I was too stubborn and proud.

"During those months at the mission I began to recall the Bible stories that my mama had taught me as a little boy. The longer I was sober, the more my mind cleared, and I came back to reason and sanity. Finally, my lifelong struggle was over as I surrendered to my Creator. I didn't need to look for my dad any longer because I had a Father who would never leave me. That was a year ago and He's been preparing me all these months to come here."

They talked for a long time. Once Sarah and Ava heard Floyd's testimony of how he had become a changed man, they were ready to open their hearts to him and welcome him back into their lives. At least they would give him a chance to be their dad.

Chapter 43

Sarah Is Back

THE FIRST PERSON Sarah wanted to see the next morning was Millie. She called her up and asked if she could come over. Millie was thrilled. From the sound of Sarah's voice, Millie was almost certain her prayers had been answered.

When Millie opened the door to her friend, Sarah said, "Let's go for a walk, Millie. The trees and flowers are so beautiful, and we can sit on the bluff overlooking the bay." As they walked through the streets toward the bay, Sarah told Millie how sorry she was for ignoring her for the past few months. "It was a mistake to date Thomas. He's just a playboy."

"Doris and Margaret asked me what you were doing with Thomas that night you drove past us at the Dairy Top. They seemed to know a few things about his track record with women. I was concerned about you, Sarah, and wished I hadn't encouraged you to be friends with Thomas. I never stopped praying for you."

Sarah assured Millie that she had firmly decided not to see Thomas anymore. They arrived at the bluff overlooking the Bay of Mobile and sat down on a bench. "But I'm dying to tell you the most exciting news of all."

The best friends sat there for a long time as Sarah told Millie all about Floyd's call and how Fan met him at the park. She described how scared she and Ava were to meet their dad for the first time as adults. After Sarah had filled Millie in on everything, Millie said, "Someone should write a book about your dad's life. It's pretty awful but it looks like there'll be a happy ending." As usual, Millie's way of putting things made Sarah laugh.

Millie and Sarah enjoyed the morning getting caught up with each other's lives. They strolled down to the bay and took their shoes off for a walk along the beach. It seemed like the good old days before the war had ruined their lives. Only now, Sarah knew she had a father in her life. She had hope that he would be someone she could talk to and lean on. He was coming to Fan's for dinner tomorrow night to meet Howard and Julia.

As Sarah walked home from Millie's she rehearsed in her mind all the things Floyd had told her and Ava. He planned to stay in Fair Pointe to be near them. He was staying at the YMCA. They had decided to hire Floyd as a physical fitness director for their exercise classes. He told them that before he'd started drinking, he'd always enjoyed a strong, athletic body. It had taken him a year to get that body back once he'd stopped drinking.

After her dad left Fan's and Ava had gone, Sarah had apologized to Fan for avoiding her all those months. Fan had hugged her with tears in her eyes.

As Sarah got close to home, she decided to cut across an open field behind Aunt Fan's. When she was a few feet from the back door she could hear Floyd and Fan talking inside. She heard Fan say, "Floyd, we can't go back and be young again. What we had back then can never be again. I've spent all these years alone and raising the girls, and I've learned to be content with my life just the way it is."

Sarah couldn't believe what she was hearing. Floyd and Fan had been a couple once? She felt very uncomfortable as she realized she was hearing a private conversation. She didn't want to eavesdrop. *I'll go back around the block and come to the front door. That way I can make plenty of noise so they'll hear me come in.*

Sarah retraced her steps back through the field. When she came to the street, she heard a horn and looked around. *Oh no, it can't be Thomas. I guess You want me to get this over with right away, Lord.* Thomas pulled up next to her with the same inviting grin he'd had when Sarah first met him. "Care for a ride, young lady?"

Sarah weighed her options and decided to get in. She steeled herself against Thomas's charms to take care of their unfinished business. She had learned that Thomas didn't easily take no for an answer.

Thomas drove them to the Bay. *I'd forgotten how beautiful she is.* He parked his car overlooking the water and turned the engine off. "Sarah I've missed you," he said. "Can't we get things back the way they used to be before that night at the Club?

"Don't you remember how good it felt to be on the dance floor together?" He chuckled softly. "People said we looked like Fred Astaire and Ginger Rogers." He reached over and smoothed a tendril of her hair away from her face and Sarah felt a trace of the old thrill.

She silently lectured herself. *Don't play with fire again. You learned your lesson.*

Thomas was waiting for Sarah to give him some hope. He looked expectantly into her eyes. Sarah hated to disappoint people and hated it even more if she hurt someone. She felt her resolve slipping as Thomas smiled into her eyes.

Help me, God. Suddenly truth invaded her mind speaking more loudly than Thomas. *He didn't change for you before and there's no reason to think he'll be different this time.*

Along with the thoughts, Sarah felt a roiling inside like the warning of a coming storm. She knew that she had to make the right decision. Her whole life was at stake. Calmness filled her as she turned to Thomas with her final answer, "No, Thomas, we can't get back together. I've turned my life over to God and He has something else for me."

Thomas had never been turned down before and he didn't like the feeling. *God? Who's he to interfere with my plans?* He wasn't ready to wave the white flag of surrender. "If I can't have you, Sarah, then life isn't worth living. I'd rather die than live without you." His eyes looked tragic and pleading.

Sarah felt rock solid. She got out of his car and calmly said, "If you take your life, Thomas, it won't be my fault. It will only be your own poor choice. I will not be responsible for what you choose to do." Thomas's countenance suddenly changed from one of tragedy and helplessness to anger and malice.

Sarah turned and walked up the hill toward her neighborhood. The old Sarah was back, and she was free.

Aunt Fan and Sarah had a pleasant dinner that evening. Fan silently thanked God for bringing Sarah back to her senses. Now they could be close again.

Later in her room, Sarah felt too happy to sleep. Instead, she sat by her window gazing out on the beautiful, moonlit night. She could see everything so plainly since she'd gotten right with God. He does answer prayer, just not the way we always want Him to. She felt a new peace and joy in her life and looked forward to going to church with Aunt Fan and Floyd Sunday.

Chapter 44

Sarah's Dream

SARAH DREAMED OF Cary again that night only this time she awoke during the dream and remembered exactly what she'd seen - Cary standing on a beach looking out over the water. He looked so normal and so alive. In the dream he fell to his knees and seemed to be praying.

Sarah knew that not all dreams mean something. But she was certain that this dream was meant to show her that Cary was alive and asking God to bring him home. She was certain of it!

This new supernatural life with God was turning out to be far more interesting than the false life she'd been experiencing with Thomas. The excitement Sarah had experienced with Thomas was like a balloon filling up with air. It just kept getting bigger and bigger. Then suddenly the balloon had burst and there was nothing left but pieces to pick up and throw in the trash.

"Good morning, Auntie," Sarah greeted. She walked over and kissed Fan's cheek. "Why, Auntie, are those tears I see?"

"Oh, I'm just being sentimental," Aunt Fan said.

Sarah suddenly remembered Fan and Floyd talking the day before. She didn't want to have secrets from Fan anymore and maybe Fan wouldn't want to have skeletons in her closet. "Do you want to tell me about you and Floyd, Auntie?" Sarah gently asked.

"How in the world would you know about Floyd and me, child?"

"I'm sorry, but I accidentally heard the two of you talking when I came to the back door yesterday. I didn't want to interfere, so I left and came back later."

Fan looked tired and resigned. "How much did you hear?" she wanted to know.

Sarah hesitated, not liking the conversation at all. "I heard you tell Floyd that the two of you can't pick up where you left off years ago. I left right away, Aunt Fan."

"It's not your fault, Sarah, don't fret. Floyd wanted to know if we could be more than friends. That's all there is to it. But he was very understanding and didn't make it hard for me. I can't imagine having a man in my life. They do complicate things, don't they?"

Sarah had an almost overwhelming desire to laugh at the understatement of the year. She smothered her guffaw and replied, "Yes, they do, Aunt Fan." She thought of telling Fan about turning Thomas down the day before, but she wanted to forget the past and move on. Instead of going into detail, Sarah simply informed Fan she wouldn't be seeing Thomas anymore.

"Oh, that's another answered prayer! Someday maybe I'll tell you about Floyd and me," Fan continued. "We were just high school kids."

"Will you be okay when Floyd is around?" Sarah asked with a little trepidation. She had faith that finally she and Ava could have a relationship with their dad, but the old fear wanted to rise up again.

"Yes, we talked about how things should be. Both Floyd and I want us all to enjoy family times together. Nothing will interfere with that, let me assure you!"

There was only one person Sarah wanted to share her dream about Cary with. She ate a quick breakfast and called Millie to say she had more news to tell her.

Chapter 45

Plans

CARY HAD COME up with a plan. He needed to talk with Cayo about it today when they were out fishing. Cary felt sure that Maria and her parents believed he would eventually come around to the idea of staying and marrying Maria. He had to get away before push came to shove.

Cary had been thinking about how to leave. It worked in his favor that he was on a Spanish-speaking island. Spain was neutral in the war. *There could be Germans on the island who would like nothing better than finding a marooned American sailor to take captive.* Cary had no idea how the war was going. He could only hope that the Allies were defeating the Nazis.

The cove these islanders called home was surrounded by inhospitable cliffs. The only way he could make his get-away was on the water. *Will Cayo help me?* Cary had become like a big brother to Cayo, but he still wasn't sure if Cayo would betray Maria and her parents. *I have everything to gain and nothing to lose by asking for Cayo's help.*

Cary walked on the trail between the two villages to where Cayo lived. The two of them walked to the beach as the first rays of sunlight began arching into the eastern sky. They dragged Cayo's boat into the water. Fish, lobster and crab were the mainstay of the islanders' diet. Even though Cary had grown up on the gulf and enjoyed eating seafood, at times he felt that he couldn't swallow one more bite of it. How his mouth watered when he thought about the nice juicy steaks he used to enjoy.

Once Cayo's trawler was out beyond the waves and away from the other boats, Cary said a silent prayer and told Cayo of his plan. "Cayo, you know I want to leave this island. You've heard me talking to Jose and the family about that, right?"

"Si, mi amigo lo se," Cayo answered.

"You also know that Maria wants me to stay." Cary hoped his powers of perception wouldn't fail him now.

Cayo told Cary that he'd seen Maria's feelings for Cary. He'd also seen that Cary did not return those feelings.

"Good, Cayo, you understand. Imagine if you had to marry one of the village girls that you didn't care for in that way. What would you do?"

"Huiria tan pronto como pudiera (I would run away as soon as I could!)" Cayo said. Cayo had a twinkle in his eye.

Cary continued, "I'm very grateful to your relatives for rescuing me and all they've done for me, but it's time for me to leave. Will you help me?"

"Lo hare!" (I will!) Cayo assured Cary. "Cual es su plan?"

As they trawled along, they formulated the plan for Cary's departure.

Chapter 46

Night and Day

BACK IN HIS hut later that day, Cary put the few clothes he planned to take in a small bag and hid it from prying eyes. He had to make sure none of Maria's family suspected anything. The four of them sat around the fire pit eating their dinner. The smoke helped keep the pesky mosquitos away. Cary thought the day would never end.

That night he lay in his bunk until he was sure Jose, Ana and Maria were asleep. He took his satchel and walked toward the beach. His heart was pounding, thinking that the watchful eyes of Jose would somehow find him. If they caught him trying to get away from them, Cary had no idea what their next scheme would be, and he didn't plan to find out.

Eventually they would see the note he'd left thanking them for taking care of him. He'd put it under his mattress. Cary usually went fishing early before the family had awakened so he was counting on having that extra time before anyone discovered he was gone.

He could make out Cayo's form by the boat as he approached. The two hardly dared to whisper in spite of the noise of the waves. Their plan was for Cayo to get Cary around the treacherous rocks and make it back before any of the fishermen headed out for their day's catch.

In less than an hour, Cayo had steered the boat around the promenade of rocks. He maneuvered the boat toward the beach and handed Cary his only map. Cary had the directions in his head but having a map might come in handy if his route had to be changed. He and Cayo had chosen the small town of La Restinga.

Before Cary jumped into the shallow waves, Cary shook Cayo's hand and embraced him. "Maybe someday you will come to Fair Pointe, Alabama and look me up, eh Amigo?"

"Lo hare! Adios. No te olvidare mi hermano."

"I won't forget you either, my brother," said Cary, then he slipped over the edge of the boat onto the beach.

His dog tags had been lost either in the explosion or the aftermath, none of which Cary could remember. If there were Americans in La Restinga, that would be to his disadvantage. But if he ran into Germans, not having the dog tags might save his life.

Cary had gotten his dark good looks from his mother's side. He'd never been more thankful. If he got entangled with a German patrol he would speak the Spanish dialect he'd learned. He could easily pass as an islander.

He had tried to think of every possible scenario. The rest was up to God.

Cary hoped his adrenaline would keep him going for the next however many hours until he'd made contact with the United States Navy. He couldn't waste a moment's time to stop and rest.

Cary started scrambling up the steep embankment. He'd looked at the map with Cayo and knew he'd have to get to the top and walk about half a mile to the road. He scrambled up the loose rocks and pushed through the many branches of the scrub bushes. Hopefully the snakes were quietly waiting for the morning sun before moving about.

When he felt like his lungs would explode, he had to stop for a few minutes. It would be a difficult climb in broad daylight. The darkness made it even more challenging. The small rocks slid and tumbled with every step he took. Finally, the first rays of dawn began to shed some light on the east-facing mountain. Cary got the map out. He took a few swigs of water which he knew he'd have to conserve as much as possible. He wasn't far from the top. If he walked directly west he would run right into the road.

Cary had asked Cayo if he should stay off the road but Cayo had convinced him that it would be too difficult and tiring and there would be poisonous snakes and wild boars. At the road he would turn south which would lead him to La Restinga. *I won't be holding my thumb out for any trucks.* Any truck approaching might be carrying sailors, either Spanish or German. *On a wing and a prayer.* He'd heard the pilots use that expression many times. Somehow the words comforted him.

Just before reaching the top of the hill, Cary heard a squealing sound. His already jumpy nerves made him leap to the side. He lost his foothold and started sliding down the steep slope. Soon his hand found a bush to grab. A big, ugly boar ran out of the bushes above him. Fortunately for Cary the ugly creature was on a mission to get her piglets to safety and well away from this clumsy intruder. When Cary's heartbeat returned to normal the sun had risen over the Atlantic.

As Cary hiked west toward the road, he thanked God that the people he'd left behind had the same topography to overcome. If they wanted to pursue him, they'd have to guess which town he had gone towards and take a small fishing boat to get there. And if Cary could get a ride from someone, there was no way any of Maria's family could beat him to La Restinga. German soldiers were his only concern. Maybe they were on the island and maybe they weren't.

There weren't many trees on top. *Not a very good place to duck out of view.* When he came to the dusty road, Cary turned south. If he judged his location accurately on the map he had about twelve miles of walking to get to La Restinga. After an hour in the hot sun, he began hoping and praying that some islander would come along and give him a lift. He carefully sipped his water and ate some of the mango he'd brought.

The direct sun and heat made his head begin to ache. *Oh, dear God, not this,* Cary pleaded. He had wondered if his head injury might flare up. Cary looked ahead hoping to see some sign of the town in the distance. He'd already used most of his energy climbing the steep mountainside. At times he thought he saw some buildings in the distance, but they always faded from his sight in the haze on the horizon.

Cary thought he heard the sound of a car approaching. He turned and looked back. There was a vehicle coming his way in a cloud of dust. There weren't any bushes or trees on this stretch of road, nowhere to dive for cover to judge what kind of vehicle it was. He picked up his pace to get to some large boulders down the road but knew he'd never make it.

My life is in Your hands, Lord, he prayed and turned to see what his fate would be. The truck coming looked like a military transport truck. He could only hope that the soldiers were Spanish. As the truck pulled up alongside of him, Cary saw the emblem on the side. It was the Swastika.

Chapter 47

Picked Up

CARY TRIED TO recall everything his drama teacher had taught him about good acting. His mind had to stay clear so he could play the part of a Spanish islander. Cary gave the Germans his friendliest grin and began talking in the Spanish dialect he'd learned.

The driver asked Cary some questions in German. Cary just shrugged and grinned. The German scout shouted back to his men in German, "What do you think? Should we give this simpleton a ride to Restinga?"

They all laughed and gave each other knowing looks. The boredom of being on the island had gotten to them. "We'll see if he can hang on over the bumps, eh fellows?" one of the men in back called out. Their raucous laughter set Cary's nerves on edge.

Cary stood there grinning at them and laughed along with them. *Keep playing dumb.*

One of the soldiers hopped out of the back and came toward Cary. He grabbed Cary's shirt and pulled him toward the pick-up bed. Two soldiers reached down and took Cary by the arms and pulled him up.

"Gracias, mi amigos," Cary said with the grin still on his face.

"We'll see how much he thanks us," a burly German said with a menacing chuckle. They'd been patrolling the island for a few weeks. It was high time they had a little entertainment.

As the truck bounced and lurched along the road, the men began their little game of "not enough room in the truck bed." They kept jostling about until Cary was perched on the end of the truck bed.

Cary knew it was only a matter of time until one of the bumps threw him off or one of the soldiers gave him a little help. *Lord, help me to land softly.* He kept up his big-dumb-man act, all the while grinning at his tormentors. He knew better than to let fear show in his eyes.

The soldiers didn't want their little game to end too soon. Every time it seemed that Cary would fall off they'd grab him and let him dangle for a few seconds before pulling him back up. Their laughter got louder with each attempt to "save" el hombre.

Okay, Lord, get me out of this situation. The driver sped up and Cary went flying off the back before any of his captors could grab him.

"Halt! Halt!" the Germans hollered to the driver. He ignored them and kept going. The cat and mouse game had abruptly ended, and they would have to look for another diversion in town.

Cary lay there pretending he'd been knocked out until the truck was far down the road and the dust had cleared. He sat up and checked for injuries. *I seem to be okay, Lord, thanks, but that wasn't exactly the deliverance I had in mind.*

Cary dragged himself to his feet and began walking again. His ears were finely attuned for any sound of trucks. He'd rather walk all the way to La Restinga than be picked up by a rowdy bunch of sailors.

He heard loud singing in Spanish before he saw the car coming. Cary ducked behind some bushes and waited to see who was arriving this time.

The jalopy had no top and appeared to have Islanders aboard. A man in back was sitting up high with a guitar in his hands singing at the top of his lungs. The two ladies and the driver were singing along and laughing.

Well, Lord? Cary felt a nudge to go for it. In spite of his pounding heart, he came out on the road to wave the jovial group down.

The driver slammed on his brakes. Once the dust cleared, Cary gave them his best smile. "Ola."

The amigos took an instant liking to Cary and smiled broadly at him. The man and lady in back scooted over and made room for Cary to climb in. Cary thought he could almost hear God smiling.

Chapter 48

More Complications

CARY'S NEW FRIENDS serenaded him with song after song. They apparently had no need to know anything about him. He tried to sing along but that only made them laugh. Finally, Cary's lack of sleep got the better of him and not even the jostling of his head from side to side could keep him awake.

When Cary awoke, he was in the jalopy by himself. People were walking past it on both sides. Cary bolted upright and had his first view of La Restinga. The sign in front of him made him rub his eyes. It read, La Restinga or as the English say, "The Set Aside." *The set aside – that's me!* He felt the urge to laugh uncontrollably but he'd save that just in case he'd have to play the part of a lunatic.

He looked around to try to figure out where to go to find a phone. Thankfully, he and Cayo had thought about the possibility of his needing money to bribe someone. Cayo had willingly dipped into his meager savings to give Cary enough money for the what-ifs.

Just as Cary was about to get out of the jalopy, he saw the German gang come out of a bar across the street and start loading into the back of their truck. Cary slumped down in his seat and grabbed the sombrero that one of the men had graciously left behind. When he finally heard the boisterous Germans fade into the distance, Cary once again sat up. *Sorry Lord, but I think I'll have to borrow this sombrero for a while.*

With the props of the sombrero and brightly colored shirt that Maria had made for him, Cary felt he could resume his acting with a little more confidence. He sauntered into the nearest restaurante and approached the bar.

"Where can I find a phone?" he asked in Spanish.

"Por ahi," the rotund barista said and pointed to a pay phone in the back corner.

Cary felt his legs shaking as he walked toward the phone. Everything seemed to be happening in slow motion, like the sluggish movements of his worst nightmares. *Just one call away from freedom.*

Chapter 49

Friendship

SARAH AND MILLIE were sitting on the Ledoux's back patio sipping their ice tea. Except for the time Sarah spent with Floyd and her family, the rest of her spare time was spent in Millie's company.

"I just have a feeling that I will be seeing John soon," Millie confided in her friend.

"I know what you mean," replied Sarah. The other day in the middle of typing the principal's graduation speech, I had to stop and pray for Cary. I knew he was in some danger and needed God's help. You are the only one, Millie, I can tell these things to. If my family knew that I'm expecting Cary to come back they'd be worried I was living in a fantasy world. But you believed my dream that he's alive and praying to come home.

If Millie had any doubts she wasn't about to burst Sarah's bubble. *And besides, why shouldn't God still show things to people in dreams? He'd done it enough times in the Bible.*

"Oh, that's happened to me several times during this war," said Millie. "I believe God nudges us when He wants us to pray for someone."

Everyone had been talking about the news that Hitler had killed himself. "We have every reason to believe we'll be seeing our guys soon," Sarah stated.

"Are you all going to the church picnic tomorrow?" asked Millie.

"Yes, we're taking watermelon and potato salad and chocolate cake," replied Sarah.

"We didn't know the Fuhrer was going to do away with himself when the picnic was planned," Millie stated matter-of-factly, "but I for one will be celebrating that such an evil person is no longer on the planet."

Sarah laughed. "I'll celebrate with you, Millie."

Mr. Evans picked the phone up and said, "Hello." He listened to the voice on the other end and almost shouted, "What?"

Mrs. Evans was always interested in who was calling. She and Jean had stopped talking and turned toward Mr. Evans. His face was breaking into the biggest smile they'd ever seen.

They wanted to ask what the news was the worst way, but he held up his hand before they could speak.

"All right, okay. Thank you, thank you so much for the call!" Mr. Evans hung up the phone and turned to Jo Ann and Jean. "Cary is alive!"

After the Evans had stopped crying and shouting praises, they looked at each other and said in one accord, "Sarah!"

They didn't even take time to call ahead to see if Sarah was home. All of them felt like they were riding on a cloud all the way to Aunt Fan's.

Floyd, Fan and Sarah were sitting on the porch after eating dinner. Sarah loved those times when she could bask in the warmth of her father's love.

They were laughing over one of Julia's latest antics. "She does say the funniest things," Aunt Fan noted.

All three of them looked toward the street as the Evans' car pulled alongside the curb. Sarah had never seen them move so fast. Sarah watched Jean get out of the back and wondered what it could be about. Her skin began to get goose bumps.

"You folks are beaming," said Aunt Fan. "You must have some very good news. Is your husband on his way home?" she asked Jean.

"Actually, he is," said Jean, "but that's not what we came to tell you."

Mr. Evans took the bull by the horns and said, "We just got a call from the Navy department. They told me that Cary is alive and well and he's on his way home."

Sarah heard someone whooping with joy and realized it was her own voice shouting to the sky. "I knew it, I knew it," she cried. "I knew my dream was true."

They were all looking at her and she quickly told them about her dream of several weeks ago that Cary was alive and praying to get home. "I didn't say anything about the dream because I didn't want anyone to talk me out of it."

Jean smiled at Sarah and came over to her. "Sarah please forgive me for getting so mad at you. I was beside myself with grief."

"I know, Jean, I forgive you," Sarah responded. "I was beside myself with grief also and wasn't making very good choices." Then she turned excitedly to Mr. Evans and begged him to tell them everything about when Cary would get home.

"I'll tell you everything I know." He explained how Cary had contacted the Navy from an island off the coast of Spain and they'd sent a rescue party to get him. "I'm sure we'll hear the details of his rescue from Cary himself when he gets back," stated Mr. Evans. "The Navy personnel informed me that Cary will call us once he gets to the states to let us know his arrival time in Fair Pointe.

There was a hushed silence as each of them thought back over the times when they'd had a ray of hope like a candle flickering in the darkness. God was still at work in His universe in spite of all the evil.

Chapter 50

Plans Gone Awry

EVERY DAY SARAH was on high alert waiting for the call to come from Cary. She assumed he would call her first and let her pass the news of his arrival on to his parents. Early in May, on a Saturday morning, the phone rang and Sarah picked it up. She had gotten so exhausted with expectancy waiting for Cary's call that she actually expected it to be Ava discussing their plans for welcoming Cary and the other sailors and soldiers back home.

"Sarah," she heard Cary's voice say.

"Cary, is it really you?" Sarah laughed.

They both talked at once, too happy to stop. Cary told her he only had enough change to talk for a few minutes and gave her his arrival date and time. "Lord willing, the bus will be pulling into the Fair Pointe Depot at 9 a.m. on May 9. You're never going to believe it when I tell you about all the adventures I've had."

"And I've got some amazing things to tell you, too." Sarah replied. Cary would be so amazed when she introduced him to her father. He'd always known Sarah harbored a secret hope that her dad would come back someday. "And wait till you meet Ava's two-year-old daughter, Julia."

Cary realized so many things had happened in their lives while he'd been away. He had a lot of catching up to do.

"We're about to begin our life together, I love you!" was Cary's last sentence.

"Yes! I love you," Sarah responded. She hung up the receiver and hugged Aunt Fan, squealing right in her ear. As Sarah took the stairs two at a time, Fan was trying to shake the fuzz out of her head.

Two days later, Aunt Fan and Sarah heard a commotion in the street outside. They walked out to the front yard and saw their neighbors running in the street waving their newspapers high in the air and shouting, "The war is over!"

Everyone had been expecting the news to break any day but to finally be able to say that it had really happened gave the American people a shot of adrenaline that broke down all inhibitions of decorum.

The rest of the day church bells pealed out the good news. Downtown Fair Pointe had closed off all the streets to vehicle traffic because of the crowds of people walking about and celebrating in the streets.

President Truman was on the radio trying to remind people that the war wasn't really over until the Japanese surrendered. He asked them to remember with solemnity all the soldiers and sailors that would not be returning home yet. But the bottled-up emotions of the American people could not be kept down any longer and the celebrations continued long into the night.

Aunt Fan, Floyd, Sarah, Ava, Howard, Julia, the Evans, the Hamlins and Millie's family had all gathered at the city park to share the joy with the people in their community. An orchestra played and everyone sang The Star-Spangled Banner.

Rationing would still be a must for who knew how long, but even the dogs parading in attendance wore brightly colored bows around their necks.

The next morning, Sarah awoke early in spite of the late night. Cary was due to arrive in Fair Pointe at nine o'clock.

At 8:45 Sarah and the rest of hers and Cary's family waited together at the bus depot. Fifteen minutes seemed like hours.

Nine o'clock came and went, then 9:30 and 10:00. Just when Mr. Evans and Sarah were going inside to ask about the delay, a man came out of the small depot and shouted through a megaphone. "The bus from Jacksonville was delayed by the celebrating yesterday and we don't know what its exact time of arrival will be. If you stay tuned to WABF 1220 the new arrival time will be announced as soon as we receive the information."

There was a great cry of dismay from the people milling about. Most of them, like Sarah, had been waiting to see a loved one they hadn't seen for at least four years. It seemed unbearable to have to turn around and go home without their loved ones.

Chapter 51

They'll Walk Together

SARAH AND EVERYONE who had gathered to welcome Cary home headed back to their cars. They agreed to listen to the radio for the new arrival time and come back to the depot.

As Floyd drove Fan and Sarah home, they discussed what could have held up the bus's arrival. "I'll bet the busses couldn't get to their depots after all the people crowded into the city streets to celebrate," suggested Floyd.

When they entered the house, her dad held the door open for them and gave Sarah a reassuring nod and pat on the arm. Sarah still could hardly believe that she really had a father who cared about her. It made all of life so much easier. She didn't know how she'd made it after her mother died. But she hadn't known then what it was like to have a dad. Now she knew.

Sarah poured herself a cool drink and took her latest book out to the porch even though she doubted she'd be able to read one sentence. Aunt Fan would keep the radio on and let her know as soon as she heard the new arrival time.

At lunch time, Fan asked Sarah to join them for lunch but she wasn't hungry. "That's okay, Auntie, you and Dad go ahead. I'm really not hungry."

Sarah reclined in the hammock and let the breeze and gentle motion put her to sleep. It had been a short night with all the celebrating. She dreamed that she and Cary were adolescents romping through the woods of Alabama together. They had built a wonderful treehouse. She had brought some dishes for them to make it like a real house. Cary had built two small wooden chairs for them to sit on. "Someday, we'll have our own home, Sarah, and you will be Mrs. Evans." Sarah laughingly answered, "That'll be the day. Friends don't get married, Cary. Only people who fall in love get married."

Sarah awoke from the dream with a little smile on her face. Her best friend was coming back to her and they would spend the rest of their lives together. And their love was the kind that lasts. *It's the kind of love that gives instead of taking.*

Sarah looked up from her book and saw Millie coming up the porch steps. "How are you holding up?" Millie asked.

"I'm all right," said Sarah. "I guess I've learned that waiting is just part of life."

"Listen to you," quipped Millie. "Now who's sounding like a philosopher? We got the call from John and he's supposed to get here in two days. I'm kind of nervous, Sarah. What if he doesn't feel the same after all these years? It's not like we'd known each other for years like you and Cary."

"Oh, Millie, how can you think such a thing?" scolded Sarah. "You've been faithfully waiting for him all this time and he sounds the same in his letters, right?"

Millie accepted Sarah's arguments as logical and decided to stop fretting.

The two girls went inside to pass the time with Aunt Fan's homemade Word game. Aunt Fan was having a hard time waiting herself and joined them at the dining table. Floyd sat on the couch reading. Sarah and Ava had discovered that Floyd had an extensive vocabulary and was an avid reader. He was a self-educated man who could hold his own in a discussion on almost any topic.

After the game, Sarah walked Millie back to the Ledoux's. Floyd and Fan would pick Sarah up on the way to the depot if the bus was soon to arrive.

Sarah told Millie goodbye and walked back toward home. She was oblivious to the immaculate yards. The birds were beginning their evening songs.

Sarah saw a yellow taxi go by and stop in front of the next house. She continued on the sidewalk and looked expectantly at the taxi to see who would get out. The car door still hadn't opened as Sarah came abreast of the yellow cab. The window rolled down and the man inside said, "Hello, beautiful, may I walk with you?"

Sarah turned and saw Cary with his dimpled chin grinning at her. "Cary, what in the world are you doing in there? Your bus hasn't arrived!" Sarah was laughing and felt like crying at the same time. *Is this another one of my crazy dreams?*

Cary jumped out of the car and they were in each other's arms. The cab driver had a big smile on his face. When Cary and Sarah's lips parted, they realized they weren't alone. Several neighbors had come outside to see what was going on.

"I didn't know our second kiss would have such a big audience," said Sarah with a twinkle in her eye.

Cary paid the driver and gave him Fan's address to take his bag to the house. As they walked hand in hand toward Aunt Fan's, Cary explained what had happened.

Floyd had been right; the busses couldn't get through the clogged city streets and all the schedules went by the wayside.

"But how did you get here?" Sarah wanted to know. They couldn't stop looking at each other. Cary wanted to kiss her again but that would have to wait.

"I hitchhiked! Do you think I'd let anything keep me from getting to you? And, by the way, I tried to call to tell you I wouldn't be on the bus, but no one answered."

Sarah laughed, "All of us were downtown celebrating the end of the war."

"Soon you will be Mrs. Evans," Cary said. His dark as night eyes held hers. "I don't plan to leave you ever again. "Let's have some kids just like us and grow old together."

"Not so fast," teased Sarah. "I want you all to myself for just a little while."

Lightning Source UK Ltd.
Milton Keynes UK
UKHW020637011220
374435UK00012B/1057